Dedicated to: My little sisters, Alex and Tracey, may you always follow your dreams.

Special thanks to: My lovely and supportive wife, Melissa; Sarah, for her encouragement and advice from conception to fruition of this book; everyone whose work made this book possible.

2

ISBN: 978-0-6151-4763-5

Edited by Jared D. Vineyard
Cover photo by Tammy Gurevich

CONTENTS

Growing up, I spent a great deal of time playing cards. At my grandparents' house it was usually Spades or Pinochle; with friends at school, Euchre was the game of choice. In all of these games it's usually a good idea to lead strong. I think this same strategy also serves well for anthologies.

Lynda Myles started out as an actress, appearing in plays ranging from Greek tragedy off-Broadway, to a Neil Simon comedy on Broadway, to *Kate* in *Taming of the Shrew* in regional theater. During a period "between engagements," she wrote a play, "Wives," which was chosen to be part of the Eugene O'Neill's National Playwrights Conference and was then produced off-off Broadway. Her second play, "Thirteen," was staged in New York and at Seattle's ACT. Ms. Myles also wrote scripts for many TV soaps and received two Emmys for "Santa Barbara." She has written for and produced segments for two highly-regarded news/talk shows on WNYC, an NPR affiliate in New York. A couple of years ago, she set out to pursue an old dream – writing short stories. She says that it's been a humbling, but incredibly fulfilling process.

At J. D. Vine Publications, we think Myles is doing a great job of pursuing that old dream. She is the Featured Author and Ace of Spades of *The Creative Writer*. I can think of no better way to begin our collection than with her story, *A Lucky Man*.

A LUCKY MAN
by
Lynda Myles

Dugan vowed to himself he would not fall into the black pit today. He made the same vow every day these days, and some days he kept it. At 90, he'd believed himself immune to surprises, had assumed the worst was behind him, and the future all too predictable. That left only the present, which he more or less viewed as a small package to be unwrapped each day and its contents used up by nightfall. He didn't think of it as a gift as some others did, but he didn't curse it either. He was determined just to get on with it.

That's why this dread that hovered around the edges of his being lately had taken him unawares. It tended to close in when he first woke up, settling on his chest, pressing down, depriving him of will and desire. The self he had constructed painstakingly since the year his life had gone off track, the self in which he had lived for more than half a century, seemed to be at risk of disintegrating, leaving – what? Back then, in the time he forced himself never to think about, he had known damned well what was haunting him. Now he wasn't sure. He used every trick at his disposal to ward it off, replaying bridge games he'd won, recalling the best sex he'd ever had, reconstructing old jokes. But it wasn't working.

He became aware of the rain pelting against the window and groped for his glasses on the nightstand. Now he could make out the bare, shivering winter branches of the oak tree just outside. He checked to see if the leaf was still there. It was. A single leaf clinging tenaciously, inexplicably, to a twisted branch. Every morning Dugan expected it to be gone, yet there it was. Waiting for the inevitable heightened his anxiety.

He reached for the cordless phone and punched in Peg's number at the hospital. He knew it by heart now. He listened to the ringing, thinking she could be in the john or out for tests, but she finally picked up.

"Hello?"

"Peg? That you?"

"Yes, it's me. Hello, Dugan."

"Your voice sounds different."

"I'm just tired. Didn't sleep well last night. How're you?"

"Fine, fine. How come?"

"How come what?"

"You didn't sleep well."

"Oh, trouble breathing. The plug for my oxygen fell out of the wall and nobody noticed at first."

"Holy Mary, Mother of—what happened?"

"I figured it out and rang for the nurse. She came after a bit and stuck it back in."

"You have to get the hell out of that joint."

"I'm trying, believe me. I've been getting a lot of treatments on the inhaler."

"I'll have to fake a heart attack so I can get over to see you."

"Don't you dare tempt fate. But I do miss our good times together, Dugan." Her voice sounded teary. He felt a moment of panic.

"Yeah, sure, everybody here misses you, too. They all ask about you." Would it kill him to tell her he missed her, he wondered? He guessed it would, because he didn't do it. "I hope you're practicing your bidding. We've got games lined up."

"I still have the book you gave me."

"Won't do any good if you don't read it, Peggy."

"I know, I will. Did you do what I asked?"

"You mean about the—"

"Did you get it out of my room?"

"I did, but nobody's going to go through your stuff."

"Just in case. Where is it?"

"Hidden in my bag, where nobody'll look. Don't forget I want to see you in it again." At last she giggled that way he loved that made her sound like a silly young girl, and he was relieved. Then she started to cough. Before he could tell her to take some water, she was coughing so hard she must've dropped the phone. He heard another woman's voice, but couldn't hear what she was saying. Then someone hung up and there was silence.

Dugan held onto the receiver and stared at the ceiling, trying to breathe evenly. He finally reached over and felt for the cradle to put the phone back. The rain kept up its constant spitting against the window pane. The goddam leaf was still flapping in the wind. He shut his eyes against it, forcing himself to think of a tough bridge hand.

But instead of cards, he saw a farmhouse, the one where he and his family had spent part of several summers as paying guests. He could see them, the husband, the wife, the young boy and the little girl – himself, of course, his wife, his children, long ago in another life – as they ran down the sloping yard from the house, hurried across the road and scrambled down the steep path on the other side that ended at bottom in deep green shade. Dugan knew this memory was dangerous, but he was sure he could stop when he needed to.

He had the little girl climb onto the wooden seat of the rope swing that hung from a high branch low to the cool overgrown earth, and had her brother jump on, standing with a leg on each side of his little sister, as he bent his knees (she ducked her head each time) and pushed his body – "Don't help, don't help!" the boy called out to his parents – until he got the swing to move, then glide smoothly, sailing out through the leaves, floating back in silence, save for the little girl's squeals of delight, as the grownups watched him dip and push and hold—

A sharp rap on the open door interrupted the reverie. Belle entered, her voice lilting with island rhythms.

"Good mornin', good mornin'! Not outta bed yet? Ya bein' a lazybones, honey?"

"No, No, I'm up. I'm up," he muttered.

"Ya missin' ya galfriend, hah?" He didn't reply. "Cheer up, dahlin'. Maybe she be comin' bok soon."

Dugan got himself to a half-sitting position and dropped his legs over the edge of the bed until his feet hit his worn slippers on the linoleum floor. Belle automatically reached out a hand to help him. "Don't help, don't help," he warned, purposely echoing the boy in the memory. Belle's hands were large and strong just like she was, and he would have liked to feel them now, on the flesh of his back and arm, even through the polyester of his pajama top, but he never gave in to pampering.

"Dat's good, dahlin', dat's good!" She beamed at him.

He grabbed hold of his walker, parked nearby, and hoisted himself upright. Upright – who was he kidding? He hoisted himself into an approximation of a vertical position, his spine curved like a roller coaster, one hip half a foot higher than the other. No matter. He was up, moving, on his way to the crapper.

"Okay, honey, whatcha gwin wear today?" Belle gestured to the closet. He didn't want her to nose around in there.

"I'll surprise you," he said.

She thought that was very funny. "Okay, okay, you surprise me."

He held in place until she walked out, deliberately not looking at the closet with the small navy-blue nylon zippered bag on the floor, his emergency kit for the hospital. He pictured the contents, fresh underwear, a toothbrush and toothpaste, Peg's short frilly red nightgown. Tucked underneath it all, stuffed into a sock was his worldly fortune, a stash of pills. He'd been holding back one here, one there, as insurance, whenever they were prescribed for this or that ailment since he came to live in this place five years ago with his brain-impaired second wife. He'd even purloined some of her leftovers when she gave up the ghost a few months after they arrived.

He shuffled the walker into the bathroom. The hodgepodge collection of medications gave him a measure of power, he felt, of control. But he also could see the humor in the situation. He imagined them all tumbling down his gullet, when the time came, tiny white discs, big yellow ones, large red capsules, small blue ones, hurrying to their respective stations - laxatives, anti-diarrheals, sedatives, stimulants, anti-coagulants, aspirin, anti-inflamatories, anti-biotics, diuretics, channel blockers, statins, all duking it out with each other in one last mighty battle. Hah!

Dugan, however, would be oblivious to these internal fireworks. He'd be gone, corpse not grata, a sinner who broke the Church's sacred law and did himself in. He still had a few qualms about burning in the flames of everlasting hell, but fewer as time went on. Enough was enough. He'd stayed around a lot longer than he would have if it'd been up to him, and if he wasn't forgiven on the other side, so be it. You could get used to anything, even fire, he supposed. Aside from the Church, there was no one left to be offended by his transgression but his daughter, and she was a continent away. It had been her idea to move him and the second wife she couldn't stand into St. Patrick's Central New Jersey Catholic Home for the Aged, Infirm, Addled and Incontinent. Then she picked herself up and moved to California with her kids, after getting a divorce, no less. She offered (only half-heartedly, he thought) to find a place out there for him, near her. Hell, he wasn't a piece of furniture to be shipped from one storage facility to another. She left, so be it. He wasn't one to waste time pissing against the wind.

Right now he wished he could piss against the porcelain. As usual it took forever for him to make his morning deposit. While he waited, one arm straight out, hand pressed against the wall to take pressure off his back (damned if he'd give in and sit to take a leak), he thought about Peg coming back. She'd gone to the hospital in the middle of the night a couple of weeks ago when she couldn't get her breath. It'd happened to her before, and each time she returned. But this stay was lasting far too long.

○ ○

A half-hour later Dugan was dressed, heading down the hall on the aluminum steed, its rear hooves shoed with gutted lime green tennis balls. He stopped outside Peg's room to look at her picture. There was a name on the wall outside each resident's door and over it a fairly recent photograph of its occupant mounted in a metal frame. The effect was cheerful, but everyone knew it was to help folks who couldn't read their own names anymore find their rooms. The camera had caught Peg at a moment when she was laughing at something. It was a nice picture.

She'd acted thrilled when he gave her the "teddy" – that's what they called it in the catalog – even though she'd turned almost as red as the thing itself. She giggled so much that he started laughing and neither one could speak for a while. Then she finally whispered, "What should I do with it?"

I suppose you could hang it from the ceiling light," he said, and they both went off again from the silliness of the whole thing. Then she took it with her into the john and wouldn't come back in the room until he turned off the lights and stuck his walker under the knob of the outer door so no one could barge in on them. He got himself to the bed and sat on the edge of it. Peg opened the bathroom door and sidled in, leaving the bathroom light on and the door open a crack so they could see each other, but not too well.

"You look terrific," he said and he meant it. "Great gams." The nightie was short, and her legs looked surprisingly long and smooth in the dim light. She was a pretty woman, would be till the day she died. She was slender, with big brown eyes. He knew the nightie was low-cut, but Peg kept her arms crossed over her chest, suddenly shy and embarrassed.

"For heaven's sake, Dugan, I'm an 87 year old bag!"

"Well, I promise, you don't look a day over 85." That set her off again, and it was the end of her self-consciousness. She sat next to him on the bed, and they talked while they held hands and stroked each other. He could smell her cologne.

"I always wanted to wear one of these sexy things," she told him, "but I never had the courage. I'm glad I got the chance before I die."

"So am I."

"Thank you."

"I'm the one who should say thank you. I never thought I'd be with a woman this way again."

"You're a handsome man, Dugan. When your wife died, the old ladies here were falling all over their walkers to get to you."

"They didn't have a chance," he joked honestly.

"You have the most wonderful smile," she said.

"Still have most of my own teeth."

She stroked his cheek. "How come you won't talk about your life, Dugan?"

"What do you want to know?"

"What you were like, what you wanted out of life."

"Not much. A good game of bridge went a long way then, too."

"You're a sphinx, you know that?"

"I thought you said I was an ostrich."

"You are, you're both. I've told you everything about my life, my marriage, my librarian job. I even admitted I'd rather read than play bridge!"

Again, he joked. "I always knew you were a little strange."

She finally gave up, as she had every time before, and they lay side by side, holding and caressing each other until it was time for the evening meal. It was nice. Not like they were twenty anymore – or even seventy – but the memory of desire was there, and at times the desire itself, even if there wasn't much follow through.

He snapped himself out of it, turned away from the photo and kept going. She's a good sport, Peg, he thought. Their only problem was that she didn't pay enough attention to the bidding at bridge. But that was about all he could say against her.

At the breakfast table, Kitty began innocently enough, "My sister-in-law Millie's sister-in-law, Jerce" – that's how she pronounced "Joyce" – "you remember Jerce, she came to visit with Millie right after my John's passin', right before I had the operation on my leg. You know, the tall girl with red hair."

That set Doris off. She was the feisty one who sat kitty-corner on his right -- or should it be Doris corner? -- with thin dyed-blond hair sprayed stiff as cardboard and too much make-up caked on for Dugan's taste. "That woman my son married has red hair. Looks like a fire hydrant."

"Jerce's hair is a different shade of red," Kitty said, impatient to get back to her story.

"I can't hear a damn word anybody's saying." Lil said. She was the little skinny one with bright blue eyes and fluffy white hair who sat across the table from Dugan. She was a nice lady, in spite of the fact that her elevator didn't stop at every floor.

Kitty gestured to her ear, "Turn up your hearing aid." Lil nodded, fumbled with a minuscule switch on the flesh-colored plastic blob in her ear. Static crackled out. "Goddamn thing," she said mildly as she fiddled with the switch.

Doris took offence. "Don't take the Lord's name in vain, if you don't mind."

"Don't do what?" Lil turned to Kitty, "What the hell did she say?"

"She wants ya' not to curse, Lil."

Lil was scornful, "I never curse. My mother raised me to be a lady."

Doris knew when she was licked. Kitty picked up her story. "Jerce is a lovely woman, such a shame what happened to her . . ." By then, Dugan was sipping his milky decaf the way he liked it, concentrating on whether he'd be able to drum up another bridge game this week before one of the current players died. It was always a race against time. Once in a while, he'd get lucky, with four players willing and able to play regularly. But it never lasted long. He finished his coffee and surfaced in time to hear Kitty say: ". . . but by then it was too late. Her bones began to snap like twigs and her frame just caved in on itself. . ."

Dugan suddenly saw the unknown woman lying in bed like a bag of broken crackers.

"Speaking of twigs," he blurted out. They all turned to look at him. He launched into a joke he'd heard on TV:

"This old couple goes back to the place where they spent their honeymoon fifty years ago, and everything's nice there, almost like it was, so when they go to bed that night, the wife says, `Sweetheart, remember the first time we were here, how you fondled me and took little bites on my ear?' The man gets out of bed without a word and starts to leave the room. The woman is upset. `What did I say wrong?' `Nothing,' he says. `I'm just going to the bathroom to get my teeth."

Lil giggled, Kitty gave a grudging smile. Doris scowled, "What's that got to do with twigs?"

Dugan stalled, "Twigs?"

"She said the woman's bones snapped like twigs and you said, `speaking of twigs.' So where's the twigs?"

"Are you sure he didn't say, `speaking of teeth'?" Lil volunteered.

Sister Veronica popped up tableside at that moment, making her morning rounds at the speed of light. "How're we all doing today?"

"Fine, Sister," they murmured, on good behavior.

Dugan always felt like a kid in Catholic school whenever one of the nuns addressed him, even when he was three times her age. Heaven help him, he had one foot in the grave, and he still wanted the Sisters to think he was a good boy.

Sister Veronica leaned in a bit and lowered her voice. "I hope you'll all be able to make it to afternoon mass today. Father Frank will be saying a special prayer for our dear friend, Peg Stepniak." Her eyes flicked to Dugan and he was sure he saw sympathy in them. He didn't like it.

"She'll be back soon enough," his voice sounded gruffer than he'd intended.

Sister Veronica nodded, "That's what we'll all pray for." Then she hurried off.

Dugan pushed back from the table so hard coffee sloshed over the rims of cups and a glass of water toppled over, soaking the cotton slacks that encased Kitty's huge thighs. She gasped, rolled her wheelchair backwards. "I'm soaked!" she wailed.

"Sorry," he said automatically, as he lifted himself painfully from his chair, almost losing his balance, catching himself on the rail of his walker. He grabbed a bunch of napkins from the table and thrust them at Kitty, "Here."

Lil smiled at him coquettishly. "I liked your joke," she said.

Dugan dragged himself away from the women as fast as he could, moving so quickly he could hardly breathe.

But he kept moving, feeling the pain in his back at a distance, separate from him. He took the shortest way to his room, and when he finally got there, closed the door behind him. Resting only a second, he pushed himself a few more feet to the closet and yanked up the emergency navy-blue nylon bag. He almost couldn't straighten up from the pain of the movement, but forced himself, doubled over, to keep going, shoving the walker ahead of him, with the bag hanging in front. He got inside the bathroom and slammed the door. Then he propped the walker under the doorknob at a tilt. They didn't have locks in this place.

Now, he was safe. He used the toilet for a seat, unzipped the bag and groped around for the sock of pills. When he pulled it out, the red nightie came with it, dropping on the floor. He hardly noticed, intent on the sock. Holding the ribbed edge of it with one hand he thrust his other hand inside and felt for the pills, closing his fingers around as many as he could hold. He was sucking in air and his heart was thumping in his ears. His hands shook so hard he was afraid to pull the pills out or they'd end up all over the floor. He needed to calm himself down, get himself under control. He closed his eyes and took a deep breath. Immediately, he saw the boy on the swing with his little sister, slowing it down so he could jump off.

With a violent shake of his head, Dugan tried to sweep the image away. He'd gone too far. Then it came to him, it didn't matter anymore. He didn't need to keep the lid on so tight any longer. Till he caught his breath and got the pills down, he could give himself the luxury and agony of remembering, at the end of this never-ending journey. Thank the Lord and pass the ammunition.

The boy, his son, Daniel -- he could allow himself to say the name, to savor it. Daniel, named after his grandfather, jumped off the swing and ran through the shade toward the sunlight. His little sister, Kathy, couldn't keep up, so Dugan lifted her and carried her in his arms as he and his wife followed the boy out into the treeless meadow where the grass was dry and sweet, mixed with purple flowers and bees that hummed around them. Daniel zigzagged around the bees, leaped over rocks, and ended up on the bank of the shallow river that had large smooth stones sticking out of it and trees that leaned out over the water.

He glanced back at his family, still crossing the meadow, then waded into the shaded water at his usual point of entry. "Watch out for the rocks, Daniel," his mother called to him, "Be careful." But Daniel knew the rocks that hid under the water and covered the riverbed better than anyone. He knew them almost like individuals, the smooth mossy stones, the slanted ones, the pointy ones you had to watch not step on. He loved the feel of the stones under his bare feet. He took his usual path to the middle of the river where he was warm in the sun again, then climbed up on the largest, smoothest rock that reached almost to the surface of the water. There he stood balancing himself, arms outstretched, giving the illusion he was actually standing on the water. His father smiled at the boy's sense of drama, feeling tenderness for his slight, awkward, sturdy body, for the child's eagerness to burst out of the cocoon of his family, his childhood, to hurry to be the next thing he was meant to be.

So it seemed almost natural when the boy put his arms together in front of him, palms down, and suddenly dove into the rippling water. But it seemed that way only for a second. Dugan's wife cried out, "Daniel, no!" They all knew the rules had been broken, even his little daughter. Dugan would have to reprimand and mete out a fit punishment when his son came sputtering up from the water, wet hair stuck flat to his head, making excuses he didn't expect to be believed, as he pulled the strands out of his eyes. Daniel would have to sit out on the bank for an hour or maybe for the rest of the afternoon. He'd have to be lectured and promise never to do such a reckless thing again.

But he didn't come up. Dugan had to rush in, slipping and sliding horribly on the slimy rocks, not feeling the abrasions to his feet and legs. He stumbled on something soft below, went under and pulled up his son's limp body. There was a great swelling gash across the forehead, blood seeping out of it. He heard a piercing scream and realized his wife was next to him in the water. Together, they struggled to get their son out of the river. The little girl was wailing at the water's edge, but Dugan didn't give her a glance. He seized a towel, pressed it on the wound, then lifted the boy higher in his arms and began to run, back across the sunny, buzzing meadow, somehow up the incline, over the concrete road and the warm grass, onto the cool porch stone, where other guests who'd been lounging were on their feet to see what was wrong. One of them, a German bachelor pharmacist, immediately offered to drive them to the nearest hospital, ten miles away. Dugan's wife staggered up, carrying the girl as they were pulling out and climbed wordlessly in the front seat. Dugan was in the back, holding his son's head in his lap, clutching the bloody towel.

Afterward, it was the imaginary scene, not the actual one, that he played over and over in his head, until he thought he'd lose his mind. The one where his son popped up from the water, laughing, where they ordered him to sit on the bank to teach him a lesson. The way it should've happened; the way it didn't happen. The child who could walk on the water wouldn't live to become a man.

Dugan pulled the fistful of pills out of the sock, hoisted himself up, and turned on the coldwater tap to fill a glass. Soon it would be over and he'd never have to be terrified again of remembering. He felt his feet entangled in something. He looked down and saw it was the red nightie on the floor. He had a sudden, unpleasantly comical vision of himself sprawled out on the bathroom linoleum, stone dead when they broke down the door. They'd turn the body over and find a cute little number from Victoria's Secret underneath. He did not want to be a dirty joke. He sat back down on the toilet seat. From this position, he was able to lean down and retrieve the flimsy garment. He brought it to his face and thought he could smell Peg, her cologne. He kept his face buried in it. After a minute he felt his chest heave and heard a moaning sob come out of himself. Then more heaving, more sobs. What was this? He didn't want this. He hadn't shed a tear in fifty years; he couldn't start now, it was too late. He wanted out now; it was time. He was entitled to oblivion.

But he couldn't stop. It was as if his entire body was dissolving into torrents of grief and anguish. Through it, he heard himself saying, "I'm sorry, I'm sorry, I'm sorry, I'm sorry . . ." over and over, a hundred times, a thousand times, he couldn't say it enough times. Sorry he couldn't save his beloved son, sorry he'd turned away from his wife and daughter – he craved their forgiveness. He was sorry he'd cheated his second wife by never loving her, and sorry he'd never told Peg how dear she was to him. The red nightie was soaked through with his tears and still he couldn't stop. There wasn't enough time left in the world to pour out all his grief.

He was in the river with his wife, his son, his daughter, in a circle, holding hands, playing a game. He could feel his son's hand in his on one side, his daughter's on the other; he could see his wife's face shining in the sun. The challenge was to keep their balance on the slippery rocks that covered the bottom as they moved around and around. When either of the children slipped, he and his wife would tighten their grip till the child was secure again and they could continue. Dugan was filled with joy. He could feel the sun-drenched river water surrounding his body.

It took a minute to realize that he was in the bathroom, not in the river, and that he was an old man. He'd fallen asleep with his cheek resting on the sink and the damp, red, balled-up nightie clutched in his hand. He was as dry now as he'd been wet before. Dry as a desert. He opened the fist that had been clutching the handful of pills. They were melted and stuck together, discoloring his palm. He reached up and turned on the cold water and let it wash away the mess in his hand. Then he gulped handfuls of it to quench his terrible thirst.

There were more pills in the sock, enough to do the job when he was ready, but first he needed to see Peg. He had to get to the hospital any way he could, so he could take her hand in his and tell her everything. Even if she couldn't hear him, he'd still tell her. Once he'd done that, he'd think about the rest of his life.

End

J. D. Vine Publications is dedicated to publishing new writers. Elli Westmorland has only been writing poetry for only about two years, but I think she is off to a good start. Previously, she has written mainly fiction and short stories. In the fall she'll be attending college to pursue creative writing. All of us at J. D. Vine Publications are behind her. She is *The Creative Writer*'s Featured Poet and we wish her much success to come.

Westmoreland's poem almost has a Hokku-like feel to it. While the writing is short and to the point, the imagery used is strong and vivid. In short, she is able to convey deep levels of emotion and paint a lasting picture with very few words.

I hope you enjoy *Shatter* as much as we did.

SHATTER
By
Elli Westmoreland

The glass beads slip in slow-motion,
Shattering on the floor
With crisp cracks as they strike,
Hail on a tin roof.

He gazes at the ruin,
The dull scarlet shards
Littered across the kitchen,
Florid reminders of his failure.

A bloody crunch
As knees slump.
A hampered sigh,
A miscarried gift.

As a little boy, I loved to pretend to be my favorite heroes like Batman or Indiana Jones. Sometimes this would involve running around with a towel tied to my neck or cracking an imaginary whip. Every once in a while I would come across a choose-your-own-adventure book. These books were great because they were written in second person, making me the hero of the book.

Second person point-of-view (POV) has the ability to draw the reader into a story in a way that is unmatched by any other POV. It is, of course, the perfect match for the choose-your-own-adventure genre, but outside of that, it is rarely utilized in fiction. The reason for this is that second person is a very hard POV to pull off.

When studying creative writing at Western Michigan University (WMU), someone would occasionally bring a story into a workshop class that was written in second person. Almost always, the story would bomb miserably. The POV has a tendency to seem unnatural and forced or it would just get tiring to read something that tells you what you are doing or what you are thinking. In the entire time of my education at WMU, I only read one such story that held up to the critiquing process reasonably well. And even that story was not all that incredible. I became convinced that writing a good story in second person just wasn't possible. Annelie Widholm changed my mind.

By making her main character also the narrator who tells the story in second person, Widholm found a way to merge second person with first person. This creative mixing of POV keeps the second person from becoming tiring. She didn't stop at mixing POVS either. This story is a melting pot of the romance, detective story, and horror genres. In this blend, Widholm manages the rare feat of making second person natural and unforced. J. D. Vine Publications proudly includes *Requiem* to *The Creative Writer*.

REQUIEM
By
Annelie Widholm

Here I stand at your threshold, my shirt slipping off my shoulders before your eyes have slid over my form. I step inside without an invitation. I put my arms around you, and love you, and have you sweep away the mundane. You are the sin and I am the sinner.

And though I know you're incapable of any deeper feeling, I can sense what it is you truly need from me. What you wish from me every time I show up at your doorstep, every time I rest in your bed and watch you stare out over a city none of us remember how we got to.

You talk of moving, but I think you can't. Not yet. Not until you're certain that what you need will not be given. You've never asked me, but I can still detect the longing.

Perhaps if I gave in you would be able to have me close, the way I wish I could be. Have me fully know all the aspects of you, not just your routines after making love to me. But you must understand that I cannot. I cannot go with you. I cannot give in to you.

I know what you are.

And deep down you scare me.

I can't leave this world to run your path.

I don't want to let you go either. I need you. I wish things were simpler. Normal. At least the normal I recognize. You . . . You can never be in my world. And I cannot enter yours the way I am now. You would have me change; you would have me embrace all those parts of me that you evoke just by being near me.

I will not.

So I rise, I kiss your shoulder, and I dress. I leave the apartment with one leg heavy and the other rushing toward the curb. I always miss you. I always return. And you know this.

Your shadow lingers against the drawn curtains and I ask myself if I truly believe my hands will be the last to touch you tonight. I know the power you're under, the craving you have. You've explained it to me, but only because I asked. I still wish I hadn't. You said you don't have a type, but a fine taste in women. You said you know when the scent is right.

My scent is too right, you told me.

And then you smiled.

You rarely smile.

And so tonight I let the predator in you loose once more. Too caught by you to have the decency to care. Too involved to not understand why you have to do what it is you do. Who will be your willing victim, my love? Who will lose their life tonight?

A pang of guilt.

It subsides, but the residue isn't pretty and I know the stains are ones I'll carry with me for the rest of my days.

Some things you don't want to get rid of.

I cross the street, get out my car key, hit the unlock button and the light inside goes on like a beacon calling me to it. Safety, warmth, homebound. I can't help but glance back toward your window.

Behind the curtains the room has gone dark. So, you're leaving then. Where do you go to hunt? A local bar? I feel my pulse elevate strangely at a thought that has occurred more frequently of late.

To follow. To find out. To see for myself.

I know what you are, but have I admitted it to myself? Fully let the realization of you enter my mind to quiver there with all its truth about myself, about the reality I live in?

I start the engine and put my foot on the pedal with a finishing clip for myself not to be ridiculous. But then I spot you: a flash of black leather. You're taking the corner, headed for downtown. I think I'm swallowing my own heart. Impatience urges me to let the feeling go as I poke around harshly within myself, stirring up the curiosity you have almost killed away and the shredded moral which is scattered around it. I come to a decision.

I slip into traffic.

□

"I always wanted to see the northern lights."

You look at me rather impertinently, as though you scoff this sentiment, before you lean over, away from me, and turn the bedside lamp off with a click. You move closer again. I'm familiar with your moods, but I had so wished it wouldn't come over you tonight. I just wanted to have some form of conversation with you, some kind of a moment that could last. But soon I must go, I know. Soon you must leave too.

I move to place my head on your chest, but you push it away. Not brutally, merely sincerely. You don't want me that near. You never do, do you? And I suppose you inevitably never will. I sigh; roll over on my side, turning my back to you. I know this doesn't bother you.

"The northern lights must be something remarkable," I grumble, feeling suddenly exhausted and knowing it is no use to consider giving into slumber since you'll only wake me in half an hour anyway, commanding I put my clothes on.

"Intense," you now say, sounding as though correcting me.

I have to turn my head so I can take in your profile: a chiseled shadow amongst shadows.

"Tell me about them," I nearly plead, hearing my own voice too late to save face, suddenly content with the lack of light in the room since I won't have to fully meet your gaze.

You shrug.

"They dance," you merely reply.

"With each other?"

You huff, but I know it's through one of those rare smiles. Then I feel your gaze upon my temple, my brow, sweeping down my cheek.

"With the wind . . . and the sun," you murmur, thoughtfully, to yourself.

Your shell is so thick. I can see it closing around you. For the first time I catch a tilt of sadness from you. It bows your neck as you look at your hands in your lap, and you are drifting. For a brief second I share the sensation with you and then you release me. You let me find my own way down, but slowly I come to rest in myself again.

I put my head back where it was before, not bearing to look at the soot-marked outline of you anymore.

It says too much, means too much, and is too clear a picture of you. Perhaps it will be the only thing I remember.

□

I drive past where I see you disappear, checking which doorway you enter, and then I continue driving down the street. I'm lucky – a car is pulling out, leaving me a vacant parking spot. I maneuver my car into it with forced calm and turn the engine off. Goose bumps spread over my arms. I'm really doing this.

I check my reflection in the rearview mirror and apply some more lipstick before exiting and heading down the sidewalk. I try my most winning smile and since it seems to fit, I wear it all the way up to the door. As expected, there is a bouncer there. My smile grows warmer. I'm glad I decided to wear the dress I'm in. He gives me the look-over, cocks one eyebrow, and then – with faked disinterest – nods for me to enter.

The sign by the door says "Mannequin".

I've never heard of it.

I enter as one would a bear's den: with extreme caution, on light feet.

The bass of the music is thumping through the walls even before I enter the large room hosting the club. I look around, taking in the people. It's a young crowd. The blessed twenties grinding to the music. I can see some thirties, though. Where do I fit in all this? In the middle, I know . . . but where do you, then? Your age is still undefined to me.

I don't belong here. I feel out of my skin. I feel like a traitor for spying on you like this.

Yet my feet have coursed out their own destination and as they have taken the first step, they will not listen to reason. And even less to sanity, as this concept has fled me, leaving a bright, blue trail behind it, as though relieved to have escaped me and my clinging ways.

I wonder how you would react if I was to be discovered. I know my life might be balancing on the tip of a knife, but I don't feel inclined to think more of it.

Walking down a wide set of stairs I enter the promised land of twirling bodies and laughter, exhilarated eyes and exaggerated dance moves. The ceiling glitters from thousands of diamond sparkles; the people glitter almost as a reflection of it. The women are wearing close to nothing; the men are enjoying it.

I walk along the dance floor, utterly transfixed by the beauty of how the dancers' movements swell and shift to the exact same beat. The room is dim and the walls look dark blue from where I'm standing, which only increases the lack of light. Spotlights are directed at the dance floor. Along the bar there are softer lights that help the bartenders show off their pretty, white smiles.

I spot you then. You're sitting with your elbows resting on the bar counter behind you, the stool you're on hosting your body effortlessly as you watch the people that surround you. Your eyes are hungry. I can see how a young woman would take it for a different sort of hunger than that which I know it is. You scan the passing ladies. Your disinterest – as apposed to the bouncer's – is evidently true. There's nothing here which tempts you.

Yet.

I swallow and glide to stand by a pillar, indeed painted dark blue with deep green leaves snaking their way up into oblivious shimmer.

Then it happens. She comes over. The girl. That girl. I see it immediately. This is it. You smile at her. So friendly, so open. I shudder. You're playing your part well. Your survival instincts remain intact; your deeply rooted appetite does as well. Though there's nothing well about it. Your finger touches her arm. She looks at it, then at you, and she smiles bashfully. Of course she's playing her part well too. She's the timid youngster who needs a bit of guidance tonight, a bit of pleasure. If you've got it, she'll take it and if you want it, she'll give it.

She just doesn't realize how much it is she'll give.

I swallow again, though the spit has completely dried up in my mouth.

How can I let this happen? I can't let this happen.

◻

"You shouldn't light so many candles," I remark as you sit down on the bed, shaking the still glowing match in your hand.

The apartment is resting in gentle light. Suspended shadows run aimlessly up the walls and try to cling to the ceiling – always failing in their task and slipping back down again. The image of my arm joins them for an instant as I move it to place my hand against your back.

You don't move, nor do you react. I bring it away again, scratching my neck and wanting to ask if you even heard me speaking. But then you wonder:

"Why?"

"Because you always forget to blow them out," I state with a smile, moving one leg to give you a friendly kick in the side.

"I like them better lit," you say.

"One of these days you'll wake up with your room set on fire," I reprimand.

You turn to me, lying on your stomach, and kiss the foot which just delivered the kick. "That would leave me terribly deformed," you say as you begin to crawl up to lie beside me.

I raise my eyebrows and look at you. The whiteness of your skin stands in stark contrast with the darkness of your hair and the blueness of your eyes. Those eyes first enticed me, long before I learned the persuasive power of your hands and tongue. Your fingers are cold as they slide across my stomach. They're always cold.

You bring your lips to trail in their wake and I close my eyes. Readily.

□

I remove myself from the room, from the vicinity of your acts, from the thumping bass and the jiving bodies. I find the restrooms and lean against the marbled wall of one of the stalls. I'm trembling. I'm choking up. I'm losing control. I'm cursing myself for always having to come up with such bright ideas. I can never let things just be what they are; I have to complicate matters further by doing this, by not being able to let go.

I gradually compose myself. I listen to the eager chatter of two girls and when I hear the door close behind them, I unlock mine and step out. My eyes land on her, standing by the mirrors. Your chosen one. Is this a sign? She's correcting her eyeliner and smiles at me – openly. I return her smile rather meekly and walk up to the mirror next to hers. I wash my hands with no real intent and then shake them instead of drying them off on a paper towel as I watch her put her eyeliner back in her small bag.

She gives me another smile, as though being two ladies in a ladies room makes us have something huge in common, and then she turns to leave. I stare at her back.

"Don't," I suddenly say.

"Pardon?" she asks.

□

"Are you asking because you're curious, or because you need to know?"

Your voice could have been trembling with the anger I can see in your eyes, but it's as gentle as always. A mere query. A simple question. But the demanding of an answer is pressing in on me from all sides and suddenly I have trouble breathing properly. It's only the second time I see you look at me this way – with disbelief. The first time was . . . long ago, if you count it in hours.

"Both," I answer you, bringing forth an adamant strength I barely knew I possessed and realizing it's there because I'm telling you the truth.

I have to know. I have to hear why I can't stay longer. Why I can't spend the night. Why you refuse to even have a look at the place I call home. Why we can only meet at nighttime and why your phone is disconnected during the day.

I am careful to keep any accusation out of my voice when I approach the issue. If there's anything I've learned it's that you don't like corners. So I'm not a girl asking a boy whether he is keeping secrets from her. I'm a lady asking a gentleman to share just a tidbit of information with her.

You observe me for a few dragged out moments. I can see how you're deciding, weighing pros and cons that are obvious to you, but that I fail to recognize. They're blurry and obscure, out of my reach, just as this lucid dream of you is. That's why I have to know what you do at night. What you do at day! To try and tie you to some sort of reachable place, where we can meet on common ground.

You sit down in the armchair by the window; your eyes haven't left my face ever since silence crept into the room.

I feel as though you're testing me. If I even blink, much less look away, I lose. I don't mind; I like looking at you.
Tell me, I urge in my head, hoping it will transfer into my gaze.
There is a pause, and then you say:
"I feed."

□

I can't tell if the woman believes me, but she looks rather frightened. She takes a step back, turns, and hurriedly leaves the restroom.

So what did I say? I didn't tell her the truth, of course. She would have slipped me into the crazy-people-drawer and then shut it tight; might even have locked it.

No, you're my brother, and *you're* the one that's a nutcase. I told her to stay away from you. I told her short stories that sounded just incredible enough to be true. I recited to her almost exactly what you have been talking to her about for the past ten minutes – you once honored me with the details of how to be successful with picking up women, in case the facts would ever come in handy. Obviously, I never thought they would. Finally, I state to the young woman that this is the way it goes with you. I'm only waiting for my father and uncle to show up and we're taking you out of here.

She thanks me, leaves disheveled. Or at least I pray she is.

I wait for ten more minutes before I dare exit the ladies room for the short corridor taking me back into the large club. I let my gaze pan over the bar. You're gone. I feel a clump form in my chest that will never go away, I fear. But then I see her, and she's not with you. She's talking to some friends with wide gestures and a pale face. They look shocked. The clump evaporates and the mist from it rises through me, settles my nerves.

Thank God.

I walk toward the entrance, needing to get out of this place. But a hand grasps my upper arm and drags me into a shadowed corner, behind a pillar and a disarray of green, fake foliage. I draw a breath, ready to scream, when the hand changes its grip and goes to my mouth. I can't see at first, but then I recognize your scent. I recognize the feel of you close, the coolness of your touch. Your fingers cease their pressure on my lips and I relax, in spite of the glow I can see in your gaze.

You're furious.

"What the hell are you doing here?" you hiss.

Your composure is unkempt and shriveled, left for dead somewhere by the bar. You're nearly shaking with rage.

"I . . ." I try.

"You're telling me that I've made a mistake," you say, voice lowered, but more clawing than if you'd been screaming in my ear. "You're telling me that trusting you was something I never should have done. You're telling me that whatever it was we had – is over. That's what you're doing here."

I shake my head feebly.

"I just had no idea . . ." I try, but your eyes flash in a way that silences me.

"I told you," you say, "everything you wanted to know."

"I had to . . . see," I murmur, tears rising from nowhere and I fight them back.

They won't be argued with and soon they slip down my cheeks. You look at me, the anger suddenly fading. A compassion I have never seen on you before takes its place. You wrap your arms around me as you lean your head with your forehead against the cranny of my neck.

"Why did you come here?" you whisper, and the sorrow in your tone makes me wrap my arms around you as well.

This was doomed from the start. Of course it was. Even when you showed me what you are I never fully got it. I didn't see how it could be true. But it is. You're a monster, a label that has been forced upon you, but one that you have chosen to accept fully. You never hid it from me. You're right, I've always known. I just didn't understand. I didn't realize.

"I love you," I whisper. "I always will."

"Do you swear it?" you ask silently.

I nod, stroking your hair when a slight pain suddenly shoots through my neck.

I furrow my brow. It feels as though the insides of my head are being pulled toward the side of my throat. Toward you. It releases, then returns like wave after wave of a sensation I can't define is sweeping through my skull. My hold on your shoulders grows tighter as the room slowly begins to dance into a blur around me. You press me to you. I feel my heart slipping, my soul aloft and put asunder. The world close and soon to be far away.

I'm beginning to grow aware.

Aware of the blood that is slipping in a thin line down my shoulder blade, as though willing to write my fate with its crimson. Aware of the suckling feeling where your lips are attached to my skin. But most of all, aware of the chilled drops that mix with my cold sweat. I have a fleeting thought that you are weeping.

Are you mourning me, my love?

I shut my eyes to all of it and wait to find what lies ahead.

For some reason an image of the sun rising in splendor, unknown to those who have not witnessed it, comes into my mind. It's tranquil and forlorn. It feels like a goodbye.

◻

"Death is only the beginning."

I look at you, wanting to say something clever in return, but at a loss for words. I know you know infinitely more of such matters than I ever will.

"I think I'd prefer it to be the end."

You smile humorlessly.

"Don't be so quick to decide on the matter."

"I know I'd prefer it to be the end," I state, resting my eyes in yours seriously.

"Eternity isn't appealing to you?"

"I believe in a different sort of eternity. Where you can rest."

"Ah, yes." An air of melancholy draws itself into your features; however, it doesn't trace them for very long, fading away as you look at me once more. "But rest is relative," you point out. " Some people need eight hours while others only need three."

"How many do you need?"

"It depends."

"On what?"

"On which part of the world I'm in."

I eye you for a few seconds; then look away.

"I want to know what lies on the other side."

"Of what?" you mimic me and I almost glare at you before containing it.

"Of death," I reply.

"Perhaps it differs for everyone," you offer.

"Maybe," I agree slowly.

"But given the choice . . . ?" you wonder and I nod. "What if you weren't presented with the decision? What if someone was to make it for you?"

I fasten my gaze in yours, feeling how relentless we both are now.

"Send me to Heaven," I say and you smile a crooked smile at that.

"But Heaven is with me. You've said so yourself," you remark.

I return your smile and watch as you walk up to the window. I rest back against the pillows in your bed and think that yes, unfortunately, it is so.

End.

CADAVER
by
Sarah M. Clinton

I am disgusted.
Ravenous wolves
and carrion crows
wade in their jealousy.
They fight over the carcass
of someone near his end.
Some disguise their intentions:
"I am a helping hand,"
waiting to clean up after
the body drops.
"I only love you; I don't want you hurt."
He's going to die,
There's no getting around that.
At least he won't be around
to witness the free meal.

"Call me Ishmael." When Herman Melville sat down to write Moby-Dick, he probably wasn't thinking, *I'm going to make this first line the most famous opening line in American literature*; yet, that is exactly what he did. It happened because he was beautifully able to capture the voice of his character, Ishmael.

Young writers are often told they need to find their voice. This phrase has become something of a cliché. Too often the voice of a writer can be heard encroaching upon his story. And when a story is written in first person, it should not be the author's voice readers hear in their heads, but the voice of the character.

Susan Coppola certainly knows how to capture the voice of a character. She chose to write the following story in first person, narrated in a dialect of English. The strong voice she wrote this character with creates intimacy between him and the reader from the very first line of the story. So go ahead and read a story I don't think you'll soon forget: *What's in a Name?*

WHAT'S IN A NAME?
by
Susan Coppola

His name's Willie Small, but there's nothing small about him. Yeah he's short, but that's got nothing to do with size. Willie Small's a giant. He's my uncle and the uncle to just about every other no papa boy in the neighborhood which includes just about everyone except Marvin Tillis. His daddy's the preacher. Mama said he only sticks around cause of the steady money and cheap communion wine he gets drunk on every Sunday night. Reverend Tillis gives hisself to the Lord in the morning then gives it up to MD 2020 at night.

Uncle Willie and Reverend Tillis don't much get along. Uncle Willie hates hypocrites almost as much as he hates junkies and he hates junkies worst than anything. Hell it's a junkie was the cause of all the trouble in the first place. Old piece of dirt named Bones Jones; most sorry ass, dribbly nosed, sleepy eyed junkie God ever spit out of His mouth. That's Bones Jones. Got the name cause he's a scrawny-butt-junkie who hardly eats; only fills his dumb self with drugs, not food. He lives, if you could call it that, in a crack house here in Overtown. Says it's his row house cause there's three burned out houses in a row on NW18th Street. The windows are all smashed; the front door all busted up and kicked in. Kinda lookin' like three guys just got the shit knocked out of them with black eyes and broken teeth leaning on each other like crooked lampposts. Least that's what I see every day I pass them on my way to the bus to Daruis Gray Middle School.

One day last month I walked by and Bones was hanging out on the stoop looking like a dirty dish rag that'd seen too many sinkfuls of pots and pans. His pants was all smeared with Lord only knows what and had wrinkles that'd make a bloodhound jealous. His shirt was open and flapping in the hot air as sticky as bubblegum; his face beaded with sweat like a shiny eggplant.

"Hey Tyrell, whatcha doin?" His words sounded fuzzy like he had a mouthful of lint.

"Going home, Bones. Got homework to do." I put my head down and started to move on; didn't want no part of Bones Jones and his crazy talk.

"I need you to get me something. It'd be worth a few bucks to ya." His nose was running and he wiped it with his arm. Uncle Willie told me to stay away from Bones, but money was money.

"Whatchu need?" I asked from the sidewalk, keeping my distance.

"I need cold capsules, lots of 'em. Come ova hea. I got money for ya." He stood fingering a clump of bills between his bony fingers, looked like chocolate licorice sticks.

"Whatcu need 'em for?" I took a step toward him, eyeing the front of the house for signs of any of Bones' junkie friends. I knew why he wanted them, just giving him a hard time.

"That ain't none of your bi'ness. Jess get 'em and there's a ten spot wittcha name on it." He flapped the money at me, waving it like a flag. I kept playing dumb.

"Okay, where I'm gonna get these pills?" I squinted. The late afternoon sun was shining in my eyes. As I walked in closer I could smell him, cheesy and moldy like dirty laundry.

"Jess go to Winn Dixie and bring your friends. Everybody grabs a few boxes. Anybody asks, you gettin 'em for your mama. I need twelve boxes, here's seventy-five, bring the change." He held out the money and I snatched it up.

"Okay I'll go after school tomorrow and see ya around four o'clock."

"I need 'em now!" He kicked at the dirt where there used to be a lawn about a hundred years ago.

"Can't--told you I got homework, besides gotta work around my Uncle Willie." Bones smiled at the drop of Uncle Willie's name. I didn't know why; didn't think to ask.

"Yeah he's a sly one your uncle. Okay, jess get here soon's you can tomorrow."

I walked back down the sidewalk and headed home. I didn't feel real good about what I'd done, but I wanted the money. Uncle Willie's birthday was coming up.

He was waiting at the kitchen table when I came in.

"Where you been? Kinda late today." His steely gray hair was stuck to his head, damp with sweat and the outline of the baseball cap he always wore when he worked. He did landscaping with my older brother Cletus; just a bustass old pickup truck with two lawn mowers, but he'd taken care of me, Cletus, and Mama for as long as I could remember.

"Bones Jones got my ear on the way home."

Uncle Willie gave me a sharp look, his copper brown eyes flashing angry. "I told you to stay away from him. Nothin' ever come outta his mouth worth listenin to, sorryass junkie. What he want?"

I had to think fast. Uncle Willie was nobody's fool, could sniff out a lie better than Mama. "Jess sayin hey, wantin to see how you, me, Mama, and Cletus was getting on." I grabbed a loaf of bread off the counter and got down a jar of peanut butter.

"What did you tell him?"

"I jess said, 'hey' and kept walkin' is all." I felt bad for fibbin', but not bad enough to tell him the truth.

"Good, you pass that trash right by Tyrell. Listen to me, you won't go wrong." The kitchen started smelling sweet from the cornbread he was frying.

"Yessuh." I took a bite from my sandwich and looked down; couldn't look him in the face no how. I couldn't wait for tomorrow to come and go so as I'd have my ten bucks and wouldn't have to mess with Bones Jones ever again.

After school the next day I got off the bus like my pants was on fire and ran the three blocks to Winn Dixie. Two of my buddies were meeting me there; we'd all buy four boxes of cold capsules. My friend Malcolm whined about Bones Jones making meth with the capsules, but he took his dollar and shut up quick enough. I started feeling jumpy when Malcolm mentioned meth, but told myself wasn't no harm in cold capsules. Besides what did I care what Bones did with them once he got 'em? Least that's how I felt going back to Bones' and collecting my ten spot.

"Gimme the bag." Bones held out his hand, long and skinny as a snake. His eyes were all bugged out and crazy looking like he'd just seen a ghost.

"Gimme my ten." I held tight to the tan plastic Winn Dixie bags, looking around for any of Bones' shady friends to come up behind and snatch them. He fumbled in his pants and pulled out a wrinkled bill, held it up to me.

"Here." I snatched it and threw him the cold capsules. The boxes and his change fell out of the bag onto the ground and as he pounced for them I took off down 18th Street like a rat caught in daylight.

With the money I got Uncle Willie a new baseball hat. Said he wouldn't know how to act with no sweat stains and grease, but he'd try. He grilled me like a burger asking where I got the money for the hat. I mumbled and stumbled my way through a story about helping out Reverend Tillis, but I never thought he believed me; gave me a sour look, a shake of the head, and walked away.

The explosion didn't happen till later that night. Damn near blew me out of bed. Cletus, who was in the bathroom when it happened, come running back in the room, his pants down around his knees lookin' like he'd been talkin' to Jesus. Maybe he was.

"Shit, what the hell?" Uncle Willie and Mama came up behind him.

"You boys okay?" Uncle Willie flipped on the light. Mama ran to my bed, started fussing with my hair and hugging me. I heard the sirens screaming down the street; sounded like they was comin' in the front door. Started feeling all squirmy and funny like I was in the middle of a naked in school dream, but couldn't wake up.

"I'm fine," I lied, but nobody was noticing at the moment.

"I'm okay, now I got my pants back on. What happened?" Cletus was smiling. This was better. Mama laughed.

"You all sit tight." Uncle Willie headed outside. Came back in shaking his head and now he was laughing too.

"Damn fool Bones Jones! Looks like he blew hisself up. Must be five fire trucks and more Metro than I've seen since the riots out there. The whole row o' houses light up like Fourth O' July. I say good riddance to the whole bunch o' them." We all ran outside. Half the neighborhood was there in pajamas watching the show. Ashes floated in the air like confetti. It smelled nasty bad like somebody'd been barbequing used gym socks. The newspapers said Bones had most definitely started a meth lab, but didn't get too far. It was good for everyone except Bones Jones and the junkies. Neighborhood was better off without them. The world was better off without them.

Everything was great until the detectives showed up. They said the store clerk recognized Malcolm. They went to the same church. It felt like God was tailing me and catching up.

They were waiting for me when I got home from school. I came in the door, threw down my backpack, and saw Uncle Willie sitting in the kitchen with two men, one white, one black, both in suits. This couldn't be good.

"Tyrell, come in here." Uncle Willie sounded serious.

"Yessuh." I put my head down like a whipped dog.

"You talk to Bones this past week?" He was drumming his fingers on the table; always did that when he was angry.

"I saw him after school the other day like I told you." My heart was pumping, my stomach doing flips like when you come over the top of the Ferris wheel.

"He ask you for anything?" His eyes, as piercing as a laser, stared right through me. I hated to lie, but I hated what the truth would bring worse.

"Nah, just spare change like he always does." I knew I'd pay for this one big time, just didn't know when.

"Nothing else, son?" The white man sized me up with the greenest eyes I'd ever seen, almost like a cat. I looked straight at him, "No, sir," then at Uncle Willie who gave me the same look he'd gave when me and Cletus started cutting up at Aunt Bessie's funeral last year. It wasn't good.

"You done with him?" Uncle Willie spoke to the black man who looked my way and nodded then he turned to me with eyes as hard as marbles.

"Okay, that's it, go inside." I couldn't believe I got off so easy, but I knew Uncle Willie wasn't gonna let me slide.

After the detectives left he called me in his room. He had an old cardboard suitcase on the bed and was untying a rope that ran around it.

"Have a seat." He motioned to the worn, nubby bedspread. "I got something to show you and then I'm gonna tell you how you gonna get square with me." This time he stared at me and there weren't any detectives around to save my ass.

"Yeah I'm talking to you. I know you did something with Bones, felt it the first time you lied to me. Tellin' me he just was sayin' hey to ya. Hell, no junkie ever wasted time on niceties. Only got time for their needs and nothin' else." He was taking piles of old brown newspapers out as he talked. His voice was sharp, but his eyes were starting to smile again.

"I'm sorry—you're right! I bought cold capsules for him. He give me ten dollars. I used it for your birthday." I figured mentioning his birthday, he'd go easy on me. He opened a paper and spread it out.

"Here, take a look at this." It was a picture of two guys hugging in some kind of sports uniforms. Their faces were shiny with sweat and they looked like they'd just licked the world with one hand tied behind their backs. I saw that one of the guys was Uncle Willie looking just like me.

"Wow, that's you; but, who's the other kid?"

"Don't recognize him without his monkey on his back, huh?" Uncle Willie fingered the paper then turned to me with a sly smile.

"It's Bones or I should say it's Ray. That's who he used to be ' long time ago. Yessir! Ray Jones, one of the finest outfielders ever come out of Central High."

I looked at Uncle Willie like I was seeing him for the first time. "How come you never told me and Cletus? Wait till I tell the guys, wait till I tell Marvis Tillis. You and Bones star sports, damn!" I was shaking my head, but smiling. I was proud of him. He cut me short.

"Never mind about spreading the news. Leave old business alone. What's done is done. I didn't show you this to brag. Showed you to help explain a few things I'm gonna tell ya." He took a breath and let it out with a sigh; sounded full of sad and lonesome. "Yeah me and Ray was something ta see. He played right or center. I was always left. Wasn't hardly a ball could be hit we couldn't shag between us. We were that sweet." He smiled, probably at the memory of some long ago grab on a hot summer day.

"Anyway, it was near the end of senior year. Scouts was at every game we played! Indians, Orioles, hell even heard the Yankees sent somebody, but never knew for sure. We were playing Carol City and leading four to one in the bottom of the eighth. They had a wicked fast pitcher on the mound name of Sam Winston. He got Ray up and in, hit him in the elbow, and shattered it. He got hooked on the damn pain pills. Then before you know it he'd moved on to crack. What a waste of a life, crying shame." He stopped talking like someone'd stepped on his tongue.

"Did you ever tryout for the pros?"

He'd taken on a whole new level of cool now. "Yeah, got to play a bit of A ball. Nothing great. Got tired of sleepin' on buses and eating out the back of every greasy spoon kitchen in the South. Family needed me too so I left after one season. Bones was already livin' on the streets when I got home. Tried to help him get clean plenty o' times. He couldn't do it." I'd never seen Uncle Willie look so sad.

"I don't understand. What's this got to do with me?"

He shook his head; gave me a look that said you've got to be kidding. "Everything, son, everything. Ray Jones was a fine good boy—best natural athlete I've ever seen and just like that-" He snapped his fingers the sound popping in the air. "He was done, end of game, finished. You gotta keep on keeping on Tyrell, can't let life creep up on you. You made a jackass move with Bones coulda cost you plenty, but you got a second chance. Bones got some second chances too, but they were never enough. Don't let that happen to you, Tyrell. Don't use up your chances." He started to fold up the newspapers and put them back in the suitcase. I stopped him.

"Can I show these to Cletus?"

He smiled. "Sure." He picked up his baseball cap and put it on. I pictured him coming to the plate, staring down a pitcher, and smacking a monster off his bat. I spent that summer working with Cletus and Uncle Willie. I squared with him for the ten spot and just kept working. By the end of the summer I had enough money to buy a plaque for the neighborhood baseball field:

Dedicated to Ray Jones and Willie Small
Life is Full of Second Chances

That fall I tried out for the baseball team at school. I play centerfield.

There are some writers that one cannot help but be inspired by. Edgar Allan Poe is certainly one such writer. I recall a particular night, not long after moving into my first apartment in L.A., that instead of forgotten lore, my only company was a volume of Poe's works. After reading a story and a few poems, I found myself stuck on *The Raven*. The rhyme scheme and rhythm of the poem was delicious on my tongue. I read it again and again out loud, relishing it. Finally, I had to write. Playing with Poe's structure was irresistible.

I stood before my keyboard that was balancing on a stack of boxes (I was too poor to afford a desk or chair at that time) and wrote the following:

> I remember it quite clearly; after nine o' clock—or nearly—maybe ten
> o'clock at most.
> Sat I there—just me only—in the apartment, bright but lonely, chewing on
> some toast.
> No one for me ever calling; I wondered if I were appalling. Then a bug I
> saw a crawling—crawling on my toast.
> Wretched thing, t' was black and hairy; at first sight a might bit scary to
> see hairy legs a crawling—crawling on my toast.
> If not for chance, with one more bite; if I did not glance, I just might had
> extra protein with my Toast!
>
> I was jolted and I bolted—involuntarily revolted—to the kitchen with my
> toast.
> I headed for the stove real quick and turned the dial just as quick and
> listened to the click-click-click till fire flared beneath my toast.
> The creature sprawling and quickly crawling, clinging and slinging to
> keep from falling; avoiding its disastrous roast.
> At my fingertip it nipped, pinching till its pinchers ripped my fleshy finger
> tip and I dropped the toast.
> Burning with a lustrous flare, I—just I—watched it there till the insect was
> a ghost.
>
> Time of year, I cant remember, whether November or December; but this I
> remember clearly, t' was after nine—or nearly—maybe ten o'
> clock
> at most.
> Sat I there—just me only—in the apartment, bright but lonely, looking at
> my blackened toast.
> The clock was tick-tick-ticking, tocking as I gently began rocking—
> rocking with my blackened toast.
> Then I began to cry and wished it were *me* to die at nine o' clock or ten at
> most.
> For I truly was appalling. Who would ever come a calling? What a
> horrible host to turn my only guest to ghost stead of sharing my
> now blackened, crispy toast!

I Can imagine Jason Kaplan having a similar experience with Poe before he wrote the following piece. This piece plays with those irresistible lines of Poe's that inspired countless readers.

Kaplan's imagination takes us behind the poetry; we glance at Poe as he tries to write his masterpiece, *The Raven*. Kaplan's Poe is, of course, highly ficionalized. Perhaps some of the Poe scholars out there will have to imagine this as the incredible coincidence of another man named Edgar Poe being struck by the same muse that made Edgar Allan famous. Or perhaps the What If Game could be played as Kaplan seems to have done: What if Poe called his mother-in-law, "Mother"? What if she hounded him to get his writing done? What if writing, not editing, was the way Poe made a living. Come on, he never made much a living either way. If you sit back and relax, perhaps take a swig of burgundy, this piece is worth a good chuckle. So suspend your disbelief and enjoy a highly anecdotal contribution to *The Creative Writer* collection: *The Maven,* written by Jason Kaplan.

THE MAVEN
by
Jason Kaplan

"Once upon a midnight dreary, while I pondered, weak and weary, Over many a quaint and curious volume of forgotten lore . . ." Pondering a rhyme for lore, Mr. Poe reclined in his leather armchair and chanced another swig of burgundy. *It's not that I'm a depressed man*, thought Mr. Poe, *it's just that nobody else seems to realize how depressing the world is.*

"Edgar! What are you doing in there? Tell the truth, Edgar, is there a single word below the margin of that page?"

Aroused from his doleful reverie, Mr. Poe hastily snatched up his quill and scribbled "word" and "some" on the first line, before turning to face the door.

"As a matter of fact, mother, there is a word below the margin, and then some."

"Really? How about the line below that?"

Taken off guard by her peculiar tenacity, Mr. Poe pivoted back to the desk and wrote another "word" on the following line.

"Yes," he replied, taking great pains to sound deeply offended.

"Seagull-scat! I can hear you scratching away right now, you little rodent! Shame on you, Edgar. As if it weren't lazy enough of you to become a writer instead of having a real job; but, on top of that you had to be a lazy writer! And don't tell me that 'it takes time to engender a masterpiece of American Literature.' That's what you were saying about 'The Pit and the Pendulum,' remember?"

"Mother, you of all people should know that Americans are in no position to judge their own literature. And besides, this one really will be a masterpiece, that is if you ever stop storming up here every five minutes and rapping at my chamber do—yes—yes, that's it!"

"What's it? What's wrong with you?"

"Never mind."

Returning to the paper with a different kind of haste, Mr. Poe resumed: "While I nodded, nearly napping, suddenly there came a tapping, as of someone gently rapping, rapping at my chamber door. ''T is some visitor,' I muttered, 'tapping at my chamber door; only this and—'"

"Edgar! You realize that I'm still here, don't you? So typical of you, Edgar, thinking that your problems and responsibilities will just disappear if you ignore them. I assume you also realize that the Baltimore Herald accepts no entries past midnight?"

"Mother, I'm really very—what!? Midnight tonight? But that's impossible! Literature takes its time to incubate in the fires of inspiration, it can't just write itself in a night."

"Actually, it'll have to write itself in about an hour."

"Impossible. I'll just have to submit it next month, that's all!"

"Oh, don't kid yourself, Edgar. You need those wages now."

Cringing half from resentful conviction and half from the burgundy, Edgar reluctantly groped for his quill, and resumed for the last time: "—nothing more. To the door I slowly journeyed, expecting peddler or attorney, rapping at my chamber door. But the mantle light revealed two floating spectacles of steel that clad a figure, well concealed, in the dark abyss beyond the threshold of my door. 'Finish your story,' the figure uttered, with an accent from the gutters, 'Or your indolent, useless figure will be strewn upon this floor!' 'T was my mother, here to press me. Wherefore lately had she blest me, now that her words held encomium nor counsel nevermore? To my chamber I retreated, the spark within me snuffed, defeated, as I fastened the great bolts and links that line my chamber door. With no dearth of angst and bale, I asked, 'Must this fate meet all my tales?' The silence answered, without fail, 'Indulge that woman nevermore.'"

"Edgar! Is it finished yet?"

Edgar responded wearily, "Yes, mother, I suppose it's finished."

"Good! That leaves you a whole ten minutes to get it to the publishers before they close. I always knew you'd amount to something, Edgar."

Gazing blankly at those four pathetic stanzas of doggerel, Edgar tensed his brow in retrospection. "There was something else there—I know there was. What was it—something about a raven? Or was it a—"

"NOW EDGAR!"

"Yes mother."

End

We all need a vacation every once in a while, an escape from our daily lives and struggles. Unfortunately, we can't always afford a plane ticket to get away from it all. Reading fiction can be a great escape. When we can't afford a plane ticket, we can pick up a book and travel to another part of the world. If that book is a fantasy, we may be able to travel to a different world altogether.

Fantasy takes escapist reading to a higher level. My dad read *The Hobbit* to me when I was a small child. My imagination went into overdrive. No longer was I a child, following rules; I was an adventurer, free and on a quest. I was right there with Bilbo Baggins and those dwarves as we traveled through the incredible world Tolken created.

Writers of fantasy create whole new worlds for us to explore. Sometimes those worlds exist completely free of our own like Tolken's Middle-earth or Frank Herbert's Dune; but often, those worlds are connected to our own like C. S. Lewis' Narnia or Roger Zelazny's Amber or Piers Anthony's Xanth. Even Harry Potter lives in our world when he is not at the magical school of Hogwarts. No matter how incredible the world of fantasy may get or how different its rules are from our world's, fantasy tales still connect with us in real ways.

Like all the writers I've mentioned above, Matthew Ryan takes us away to a fantastical world in the following story. Yet he knows that a story, no matter how rich with fantasy, must be about something real. It is human emotions that drive the characters forward in all fantasy books. Ryan picked one of the strongest emotions of all to make his story about: love. So prepare to escape from your world into Ryan's as you read *Sacrifice*.

SACRIFICE
by
Matthew Ryan

She is beautiful, Daravin Hilburl thought. She stood at the top of the Meeting Rock. Her golden hair hung loosely at her shoulders glittering in the light of early morning and her amber eyes shone like small gemstones. She was tall for a female shaladryn, nearly three and a half feet in height. Her face was well-rounded, with a pudgy chin and pudgy throat. She was dressed in the skin of a leopard, all yellow, orange, and white, with a spattering of black spots. The leopard skin covered her torso and her waist, but left her arms exposed to the sun. The hair along her forearms and wrists was light and downy and suggestive of a gentle, soothing touch.

On the right hand side of her body, three blue feathers depended. Her othwan, as such was called, marked her as a young Clan Mistress. The fact that she had three sacred feathers hanging from her side—instead of the normal two—denoted her high rank. Each feather was adorned with kritsen, the sacred beads of life-telling. The first feather told the story of her life and the second told of her friends and enemies. Indeed, she had set a special blue stone on her second feather to represent her friendship with Daravin (a pink bead representing love would have drawn unwanted attention). Perhaps he should be happy: very few commoner's were even mentioned in the othwans of the leaders. But he was not happy. The third feather, the one that set her apart, recorded her experience as a leader of her people. Since she was sixteen and inexperienced, it was very nearly bare. Daravin's sacred othwan, had only two feathers; he was just a tanner, a commoner.

And the difference of a single feather kept them worlds apart.

Her name was Avaria Bearclaw and she was the Clanmaster's daughter. And as an early morning vision, she was utterly unforgettable.

From four rows back in the gathering ranks of the shaladryn people, Daravin stared in near-awe at the young Clanmistress. They were the right age for each other, each being sixteen years old, but they were from two different worlds when it came to social class. She could no more marry him than a leopard could eat a rock.

But he had given her his heart in the secret hours before the dawn. They had lain in each others arms and talked of fanciful things, of a bright future free of castes and social propriety, a time when they could love each other openly and without fear. But such a time was just a dream, a dream they both shared but still no more real as a result of that fact.

Daravin sighed to himself. They had kept their love a secret from all but his best friend, Galarian. That was their sacrifice. While she was still alive, his mother had told him once, that love demanded sacrifice. If one wasn't willing to put the needs of your beloved before your own, then it was not "love", but rather something more vulgar. The secrecy was the struggle of their love; it proved their willingness to sacrifice for each other. And surely it was a struggle. They lived each day with the fear of being exposed. Such exposure would bring great scandal to the shaladryn. Either one or the other, or perhaps even both would be driven from the clan. They would become Outcasts. Dead, as far as the other shaladryn were concerned. So they kept their love a secret. And a secret it would remain. He knew Galarian would never tell--he had sworn his friend to silence. And Galarian was a very trustworthy fellow.

Atop the Meeting Rock, the Clanmaster was ready to speak to the gathered shaladryn. He waved his staff above his head for silence. "Greetings, my people," he said, and the hushed whispers and low-level talking subsided. "We have come together today, with joyous hearts and thankful lips. We honor Halfast the Quick and the taming of his great eagle, Brightwing." A wave of cheers spread across the crowd. "Today is the Festival of Eagles; it is a time to mark and remember our kinship with all living creatures. It is time to celebrate our close relationship with the blessed birds of the air with whom we speak, and laugh, and sing. This year is extraordinarily special: our head priest, Wickaran Grasshunter, is prepared to choose a new apprentice. Only one shaladryn will be chosen. In order to be chosen, he or she must tame and ride one of the Ethrim during the Eagle's Dance." There was a murmur of excitement at this announcement. The Ethrim were the great eagles, creatures with wingspans over twenty feet long. They were secretive creatures. Only occasions of great importance brought them down from their eyries in the heights of the western mountains. The choosing of the head priest was one such occasion. The head priests's apprentice was a much sought after and much honored position in the Clan. With it came many great responsibilities and
priveleges.

Clanmaster Roderick Bearclaw held his staff above his head. Silence spread among the gathered shaladryn. With a quick, fluid movement he brought his staff down in front of him and rapped it on the top of the Meeting Rock. "Let the celebration begin!"

To his left, Daravin's friend Galarian reached out and patted him on the shoulder. "It could be you," Galarian said. "You know as much about our religion as anyone, you are great with birds, and . . ." His voice dropped to a whisper. "You have great cause; as apprentice to the head priest, you'll be allowed to court the Clanmaster's daughter."

"If only I was that lucky," Daravin murmured in reply. He felt his heart sink. The gods were torturing him with his love. Holding it out like a carrot to drive him forward. They were getting his hopes up, making him think that he had this one last chance of fulfilling his dreams, but all the while preparing to dash those dreams to dust. *I will never succeed*, he thought. *Our love will remain a secret, or worse, become a scandal and I'll be driven into the outer lands.* No matter how careful they were, the truth was bound to be found out sooner or later.

The crowd of shaladryn moved forward, parting in two streams around the Meeting Rock. They moved beyond it about thirty yards, then the dancing began. First were the Bloodstone Warriors, the fighters of the clan. Most of them were male. Each of them, whether male or female, had a deep red bloodstone partway down the first feather of his or her othwan.

The first bloodstone warrior placed a large, fist-sized stone in the center of the Summoning Field, the field beyond the Meeting Rock where the great dance was to be held. With a flourish, he drew out his short sword and made a small cut across his left forearm. He let two drops of blood fall on the stone, then he lifted his hands up to the heavens and danced in a circle around the stone. After circling the stone tightly three times, he moved off to a greater distance, giving others room to approach the stone while he continued to dance. The next bloodstone warrior approached the stone and did the same thing, putting his own stone down and dripping his own blood across it. The other warriors followed in turn.

Soon there was a small pile of rocks, sprinkled with blood, around which nearly thirty warriors danced in a circle. That's when the eagles began to arrive. They flew in from all directions, coming down from the clouds and across the land from the high hills to the east, west, and north. Large and small they came: eagles of every shade and color. But alas, there were no Ethrim, none of the great eagles. None of the bloodstone warriors would be chosen to become a priest.

Next came the Clansmen, both male and female. They were the adults, those who had performed the Eagle's Dance before, be it merely once or as many as fifty times. One by one they moved out to the pile of rocks and tossed additional rocks upon it. They danced in three tight circles, then moved back to dance among the bloodstone warriors. There were nearly two hundred dancing shaladryn now, moving in a great ring about the rock pile. Circling in the air above, hundreds of eagles soared, watching the festival from their great height and cawing in delight. Still, no Ethrim had made an appearance.

Now it was time for the Inititiates, those of the shaladryn for whom this was their first Eagle's Dance. It was their coming of age ritual, a day of choosing for both them and the clan. After today, if they passed the test, if they were chosen by the birds of the clan, they would be adults, bearing all the responsibilities and enjoying all the privileges that came with such a distinction. If they failed, if no bird answered their summons, they would be driven from the clan forever. There were eleven of them. Daravin and Galarian and even Avaria were among them. The first of the eleven moved forward and Daravin felt his heart flutter in his chest. Even though his head knew his cause to be hopeless, he could not quell the surging hope in his heart. It was nearly time. Time to prove his worth to Avaria and her father. Or to fail utterly and be driven from the Clan.

As the first of the Initiates danced around the rock pile, an eagle, a normal sized one, dropped from the sky and landed. The initiate approached and picked the eagle up. It stood on his right forearm, then cawed in pleasure. It had chosen him, and he had chosen it. He lifted his arm high, the surrounding clansmen cheered, then the eagle released its hold and ascended into the sky.

"Looks like Moravin has been allowed into the clan," Galarian said. Daravin's friend was still close by, close enough to be heard anyway. "I can only hope that the same courtesy will be allowed for me."

The next initiate went. It was a young female shaladryn dressed in coyote fur with brown hair and sparkling blue eyes. She danced around the rock pile with great vigor and enthusiasm. But no eagle descended. She danced in a cunningly crafted pattern with the skill of an artist. But no eagle descended. She quickened her pace, her face now becoming a frightened mask. Tears began streaming from her eyes. But still, no eagle descended. When she was finished, she bowed her head in utter misery. She had become an Outcast, rejected by the clan and its birds. There was a murmur of contempt from the surrounding crowd of shaladryn, then she turned and began walking away, out of the circle. She had the rest of the day to pack up her belongings and then leave the land owned by the clan, never to return. And she would leave in silence. Not even her parents or her siblings would ever speak to her again.

The other initiates followed.

Daravin watched Galarian perform the ritual; he was delighted when an eagle descended to his friend. Galarian had passed the test; he was now an adult of the clan.

Soon it was Daravin's turn. His heart began to beat rapidly. So much hung on the line with this dance. Would he be dismissed as an Outcast? Or, would he summon an Ethrim? Or would he merely gain acceptance by summoning a normal bird? He approached the rock pile and began to dance. He felt the rhythm of the secret music in his bones. He could feel his spirit calling out to the heavens, speaking with a voice of thunder to the clouds. Something responded. Something was moving toward him from above, descending through the sky on powerful wings. He stopped dancing as a shadow moved over him. A gargantuan bird descended amidst the shaladryn. It was too big to land on the rock pile, so it landed in the field.

Daravin could not believe it. His heart leapt for joy.

Words came unbidden into his head. *Greetings, young shaladryn.* Daravin started in surprise. He did not know that the Ethrim were capable of such, speaking without words, mind to mind. *Do not be afraid, young shaladryn. I will not harm you. You must climb upon my back and I shall show you the skies.*

There was the sound of roaring around him. It took a moment for Daravin to recognize the roaring as cheers from the crowd of shaladryn. His heart beating fiercely in his chest, he approached the Ethrim. Looking back, he saw Avaria's face beeming with pride and hope. He felt a tingling sensation throughout his body. The great bird sat on the ground, lowering its shoulder to him. He gripped several side feathers and crawled up onto the creature's back.

He had just situated himself on the back of the bird when it stood on its taloned feet and launched itself into the sky.

The wind rushed past him. He felt his stomach drop into his toes. The rock pile, the dancing ring of shaladryn, the Summoning Field, all dropped away beneath him. Soon he was up in the sky, a mile high or more. He could see the other eagles, small delicate birds in comparison, flying about him: they gave way to the Ethrim, flying to either side of the great bird.

With powerful strokes of its wings, the Ethrim flew south. *I shall show you the lay of the land, your land, that you now serve.* In Daravin's mind, the Ethrim voice was crystal clear against the roaring of the wind.

I can hear your thoughts, can you hear mine? Daravin thought in his head. He waited expectantly, not sure if there would be an answer.

Yes. With a little effort, I can hear everything that goes on in your head. Daravin did not quite know what to make of that. At some levels that was quite disturbing. After all, everybody wanted some kind of privacy. And what could be more private than one's own personal thoughts.

Am I allowed any secrets from you? Daravin asked.

I'm afraid not.

Daravin thought about Avaria and his feelings for her. Those feelings would not be well received by her father, Roderick. After all, Daravin was only a lowly... No, that had changed. He was so used to feeling that his cause was hopeless, he hadn't thought much about his new position. He was to be the head priest's apprentice.

Is that what you want? the Ethrim asked.

Daravin started. It was so easy to forget that the Ethrim was still in his head. *I really just want Avaria. I will be the head priest's apprentice if I can have Avaria at my side. She has the heart of an Aspallan priestess and beauty to match.* The order of Aspallan priests and priestesses were well known for their compassion and kindness. Cult members were usually human in race, but they often sent missionaries among the shaladryn people. They were well-regarded by nearly everyone who met them.

I see, thought the Ethrim. *Does she feel the same about you?*

Yes, Daravin thought back. *We see much of each other, but only in secret. It is against tradition. We have different stations.*

Then now it falls upon you to act. You can keep your love a secret no longer. You have shattered the limitations of your former caste. You must proceed.

The Ethrim flew south for nearly a quarter of an hour, its powerful wings covering many miles at a great rate. They traveled deep into the Shaladryn Hills, until at last they came upon a great ravine that scarred the land. It ran east and west along the edge of two great, rock-covered hills. A small herd of goats were moving along the edge of the ravine, heading east to the mountains. *This ravine marks the end of your territory to the south. The edge of those mountains marks the end of your territory to the east. Now we must head west to the river.*

The Alspeth River? Daravin thought in reply. *I've been there before.*

Yes, the Alspeth River. It and its tributary to the north mark the end of your people's territory to the west and to the north. But if you have already seen them, we shall return to your clan. They shall be missing you.

I don't mind if we fly for longer. I can see the river again. Daravin did not quite want to return just yet. To return meant that he would have to face Avaria's father and tell him the truth. It was still within Roderick's power to reject him. He could only court Avaria if Roderick agreed to it. He would have to expose his heart, and live with the consequences. He swallowed nervously.

The thoughts of the Ethrim sounded amused. *Do not put off what you must do. If she is destined to be your mate, you must speak with an honest heart. We shall return to your clan. You will do what you must.*

The Ethrim turned in a half circle and headed back to the north. Daravin nervously fidgeted while clasping tightly to the feathers on the bird's back. He tried to control his breathing, but it was coming fast and furious as the anxiety enfolded his heart. He felt like there were ants inside him and his skin was about to crawl away in every direction at once. Soon he was wishing to be back with the clan just so he could do what he had to do and get it over with.

Daravin looked down at the circle of dancing shaladryn. Although they still danced, they awaited his return. No other shaladryn had approached the rock pile in his absence. *They seem so small from up here,* he thought. Then the Ethrim began to descend. The little specks that were the shaladryn people began to grow. The Ethrim landed near the center of the ring of dancing shaladryn, slightly to the side of the central rock pile.

It is time to disembark, my young shaladryn friend, thought the Ethrim. The bird turned its massive head to the right so that it could peer at Daravin out of one big, beautiful, blue eye.

Daravin looked back into the depths of that eye and felt like he was staring into a pool of water. He said, "Tell me your name, before I go. I would like to know."

It is Karnar, my young friend. And fear not, we shall meet again. You will not be forgotten.

Daravin climbed off the bird's back, holding onto two incredibly large feathers as he slid down the creature's shoulder. Only when he was safely on the ground did he let go and pat the bird affectionately on the shoulder, or as high up toward the shoulder as he could reach.

He moved to the outer ring of dancing shaladryn as the great bird ascended into the sky once again. He began to dance, joining in with the throng. It was Avaria's turn next. He would wait until after the ceremony to speak to Roderick.

Avaria danced around the rock pile, every motion of her body filled with grace and poise. Daravin almost stopped his own dancing to watch her, he was so enamored with Avaria's movements. But Galarian was there; he nudged Daravin and spoke a harsh word in his ear, and Daravin started up once again.

As Avaria danced, the expression on her face changed. It turned from one of excitement and pleasure, to one of fear and trepidation. She danced and she danced, her movements becoming more desperate with each step she took. It soon became obvious that no bird was descending to greet her. She was under the same onus as the other Initiates: if no bird showed, she could not join the tribe. She was Outcast.

Daravin watched in horror as she collapsed on the ground, bursting into tears. Suddenly, he found himself in a bitter reversal of fortune. He was to become a shaladryn priest. She was an Outcast, the lowest of the low. How could he marry her now?

After several moments of sobbing, Avaria rose to her feet, wiped her face with a grubby hand, and began to walk out of the circle, gathering as much dignity and poise as she could muster. She cast a furtive look in Daravin's direction. Their eyes met. For a moment, he held her gaze; her eyes were filled with pain and longing and shame.

He thought back to his mother and her words of wisdom: "All love demands sacrifice." If one wasn't willing to sacrifice one's own needs for the needs of another, then it really wasn't love. It was something else, something unworthy of the title "love".

Before he even realized what he was doing, Daravin had stepped out of the circle and began walking towards Avaria. He had waited so long for a day like today, a day when he would be worthy of her. Now that day had come, and in a cruel twist of fate, she had been thrown into the ranks of the Outcast. But to him, that did not matter. She was still Avaria. She was still the young shaladryn woman he loved. And he would not let her go without a fight.

He called her name as he approached, and she stopped where she was. It was forbidden to speak to Outcasts.

He called her name again, and she turned around.

"Do not speak so to me, sir," she said. "I am unworthy. I am a creature of the dust, a serpent in all but form."

"I will speak to you as I please, none control my tongue but me." Daravin was vaguely aware of the other shaladryn watching them. He heard a murmur of disapproval run across the ranks. He didn't care. It had never been his desire to become just a priest, although becoming such would be a great honor. He knew what he wanted, and she was standing right in front of him.

"Why do you speak to me? I must go. The birds have chosen and I am unworthy," she said. Yet even as she spoke, Daravin saw a light of hope in her tear-filled eyes. This was the moment he had dreamed of for so long. It was not exactly the way he had envisioned it. But it was that moment, nonetheless.

"Why?" he asked. "You are my friend and my love, and I cannot leave you to face the cold, cruel world alone."

Tears streamed down her face. She reached toward him and he reached toward her. They embraced. There before the shocked anger of their people, they professed their love. Daravin sighed. He would never be a priest now, but that did not matter. He had what he wanted. He would be an Outcast, and all was well.

End.

SELF-INFLICTED
by
Jessie May Murray

She resents what she deems as intangible demons
But not before stopping to caress their napes;
They are only the shadows of moments
Random shapes
That symbolize what she wishes she had not so enjoyed

She imagines herself fighting a really good fight
One she thinks she has the power to win this time
Her intentions are good, omniscient, sublime
She believes she deserves what she keeps on getting

She believes by recognizing patterns she can stave off the inevitable
And she didn't even hear what she just said out loud
She is scared; she is able; she is pretty; she is proud
She is mourning what's missing and feeling the void

She is trying, she tells them, and shakes angry fists
At a crowd that is paying her little to no mind
They are watching the dancers who are deaf, dumb and blind
And her rhythm and theirs seem unnaturally intertwined

Why then, in this instance, does she pick at her feet
And draw blood from her veins and spew rancid on the floor?
Is she trying to tell them that she must find the door?
Or does she want, good or bad, to be watched a litttle more?

There are many weapons in the arsenal of the creative writer from the bullets of listing to the guns of metaphor. Chris Medaglia decided to see how far personification could take him in attacking a piece.

Personification is exactly what it sounds like; it is giving the traits or qualities of a person to something that is not human. Fiction writers often use personification to add depth and tone to their descriptions of places or things in a story. Used well, this writing weapon can basically turn things like a house or a car into another character inside a story.

It is not everyday you read a piece that takes personification as far as Medaglia decided to take it in *What If.* Here is a piece of flash fiction created entirely through personification.

WHAT IF
by
Chris Medaglia

An ancient tree stands at the edge of a great forest, slightly apart from the neighboring trees. Outwardly, the tree seems strong and virile, its bark crusted from years of growth and weather, its branches gnarled and still covered with gray-green leaves. Inside, its heart grows ever darker, eaten away by the long, lonely years.

It stands far enough away from the forest that its neighbors have long forgotten it. Its leaves sigh in the breeze, longing for companionship. Its face is turned away, always looking at a hill in the near distance. It spies a tree it never noticed before, just beyond the hill in the next forest, its glistening white bark and slender trunk giving way to a gorgeous complement of green leaves, shimmering in the distant breeze.

The far off tree seems to beckon, reaching out, inviting with its branches. Could the ancient tree move, it would drag its tired roots across the fields and over the hill to be near a tree so lovely as this. Its roots are deep, and a lone sapling has grown next to it, sheltering itself in the shadow of the ancient tree. The far off tree can do no better, rooted as it is in its own rocky soil, happy but incomplete, wanting for more than the neighboring trees can give.

The two trees exchange furtive sighs, for the distance is too great and they will forever be unable to hear the other. Their leaves appear to wither at the prospect as the sky turns gray with the threat of snow. Years will pass and they will forget in time. The ancient tree will eventually die off, leaving only a shell of broken bark.

The far off tree will gaze across the fields in sorrow, shedding leaves in an offering of love for the ancient tree. The far off tree will continue on, becoming empty, cold and dark as the years pass, wondering what if, what if. No answer comes, only the bitter wind of winter and a blanket of snow around its roots.

While at Western Michigan University, I had the fortune of studying fiction writing under Stu Dybek. I was excited to get the chance to learn from such a respected and successful writer; however, the first story I submitted to be workshopped in his class was a rough draft. Bad idea. Dybek's red pen was all over it. He said I was a good storyteller, but my piece showed very amateur writing.

Determined not to let the same thing happen again, I dug up an old story of mine and began the rewriting process on it. I rewrote and rewrote until I had a draft that was not only completely different from the story I began with, but was written with very carefully constructed sentences.

Different efforts produce different results. In this particular case, I ended up with one of my most memorable moments. Dybek described the language as "razor sharp" and told me that with this piece I was not only a storyteller, but a writer. Now I present the story for your consideration; it is named *Aural*.

AURAL
by
Jared D. Vineyard

~This is not a love story; it's a stalker story.~

No, it's just what happened.

~You thought Angela Errington was pretty. You started stalking her.~

To be honest with you sir, I didn't think Angel was very pretty.

~Angel? Angela Errington?~

Angel Errington.

~You didn't think she was pretty?~

No, not really. She was plain, with straight, brown hair, slightly freckled skin, and a body that was too skinny. Her looks were not what drew me to her. I think it was her voice that did it. Yes, it was her voice. I couldn't get it out of my head. The lovely tone that she spoke with, it seemed to flow out of her. It mesmerized me. I'll never forget the first words I heard her speak . . .

"Third floor, please." She adjusted her sunglasses as she spoke to me.

I pushed the button and the elevator began its ascent. I kept glancing at her out of the corner of my eye. She had backed all the way into the corner of the elevator. Her arms were crossed. Occasionally, she reached up to adjust her sunglasses, but as soon as she was done, she'd cross her arms again. I couldn't see her eyes at all, so I wasn't sure if she could see that I kept glancing over at her. Every time I snuck a peek, I made it shorter than the one before. Her voice was ringing in my head. Third floor, please . . . Third floor, please . . .

Ding. The elevator stopped.

~Do you really need to make sound effects?~

Do you really need to hear my story?

~I'm sorry. Please continue.~

Where was I? Oh yeah . . . The elevator stopped. I looked at her, turning my whole body this time, as she stepped out. The doors shut and I was left alone with the sound of her voice echoing in my head. Third floor, please. . . The elevator climbed to the fourth floor. . . Third floor, please. . . Fifth floor. . . Third floor, please. . .

Ding.

~What? I didn't say anything that time.~

You looked at me funny.

~Just keep going.~

Stepping out into the hallway of the fifth floor, I wished I lived in one of the third floor apartments. I wished I had talked to her. I didn't say anything. Of course I didn't say anything; I never say anything. As I look back on it, I'm sort of glad I didn't say anything. If I had, her voice might not have been echoing in my head. It was soft and gentle as her words created a melody in my brain.

~What was? Angela's voice?~

Angel's voice! Yes! Pay attention. My own voice was nowhere to be found. That was a good thing. People always said my voice was monotone, so I never used it much. My own parents told me that my voice was wretched. My whole life I was stuck with this terrible voice in my head; but suddenly, there was a beautiful voice there to replace it. This new voice made me run to my apartment as it sang a lovely melody. I couldn't bare the thought of losing that melody she had created in me. It took only a few seconds for me to get to my keyboard and play the song that was her.

~All she said was, "Third floor, please."~

You're not a musician are you?

~No.~

I saw her again a couple days later. I tried to speak, but my mouth wouldn't let any breath out. My palms started to sweat in my pockets. It was our second meeting inside that little elevator. This time, she had entered first. From behind those sunglasses she wore, she asked, "What floor?" Her melodic voice sent an ice pick down my spine and a wooden block to my throat. Slowly, I raised my sweaty hand to reveal five trembling fingers. She pushed the button and the elevator took us.

~For a guy who claims not to talk much, you sure are long-winded.~

You said you wanted me to tell you everything.

~Yeah, I did, but I only need the details of July the fifth.~

That's not everything!

I'm giving you the whole story, not just the little portion that you preoccupy yourself with.

~Okay, keep going. I won't interrupt.~

As we ascended, she studied the floor. Her arms were crossed, just like the last time we shared the elevator. Then she began to hum. She was ever so quiet at first; I could hardly hear the beautiful sound. As the third floor approached, her melody grew stronger. My tensions and inhibitions floated away as her voice gently caressed me.

Ding.

The music stopped. My heart stopped. She was stepping off the elevator and I was soon to be alone. "What song were you humming?" I spoke very flat, without inflection. I hated my voice. You could hardly tell I was asking a question by listening to me speak.

"I'm sorry," she said with that gentle voice. "I didn't mean to bother you."

"No. You didn't bother me," I stammered, still very monotone. I could feel myself tensing up again. My stomach was tightening and it was difficult to force air out of my chest.

The elevator door closed. I was alone and the last voice I heard was my own. I slunk back against the wall of the elevator. I tried desperately to hear her voice, but it was gone. All that was left was my own. I couldn't even figure out what song she was singing.

Ding.

~You could at least try to make those dings sound a little bit different than your normal voice.~

You said you wouldn't interrupt.

I slowly made my way to my apartment, brushed my teeth, stripped to my T-shirt and underwear, and got into bed. Eventually, I fell asleep to the sound of my tedious voice beating against the walls of my brain.

The lights were pretty low the next night at Lou's Bar. It was a good thing I didn't use sheet music because I probably couldn't have read it. To be honest, I can't read sheet music anyway; I play by ear or make up my own stuff. Striking those white and black keys on Baby Grande brought me joy. It was about the only thing that brought me joy. I breathed in the music that seemed to flow naturally out of the piano. The music was thicker than the cigarette smoke. Every once in a while I looked out at the people, sitting at tables and booths. None of them seemed to notice I was there, but it didn't matter to me. I just played and breathed.

After finishing a song, I rubbed all of my knuckles. One by one, each knuckle got its massage. My hands shook and I winced as I touched each finger. In an attempt to divert my attention, I took another look at the tables. There weren't many people in the bar that night. A few drunks here, a couple social drinkers there . . . Then I saw Angel.

She sat at a booth, across from a man I had never seen before. Those sunglasses were on her face, as always. The man that was with her drank heavily and spat when he talked. She was practically getting a shower sitting across from him. She didn't seem to be doing any talking at all.

As I realized I was staring, her head turned in my direction. I gasped in too much air mixed with saliva, and felt the urgent need to cough. I lowered my head to look at the keys and held back the coughing for as long as I could. It wasn't very long. I began hacking up a storm. I couldn't stop coughing. The coughing slowed for a moment and I reached for my water. After a couple swallows and a few slow breaths, I got myself under control. My throat still tickled. I looked up again at the booth she was sitting at. The table had some empty glasses on it, but the booth was empty. She was gone.

I looked at the keys of the piano in front of me. Just as I was about to strike a new chord, I heard, "Hey, aren't you the guy from the elevator?"

I spun around on the bench and she was there speaking to me. How I loved that voice. As she stood there, her arms were not crossed, but by her side. She almost looked relaxed. "It is you," she said.

The natural melody she spoke with made me forget the world around me. "Yeah, it's me," I said.

"I didn't know you were a musician."

I didn't know what to say. I was pretty nervous. There was an awkward silence.

She broke it, "Maybe you could play a song for me."

I swallowed and responded with a shaky voice. "Yeah, maybe. Would you like me to play the song you were humming on the elevator?"

"Could you? It's my favorite song." She sounded excited.

I was excited. "Maybe I could. I still don't know what song it was."

She smiled. It was the first time I had ever seen her smile. She might have been plain, but her smile wasn't. Her smile was beautiful, like her voice. Just as she started to tell me the name of the song, a hand grabbed her arm. She was pulled violently away from me. Her sunglasses flew to the ground. The man who was sitting with her stood where she was. He glared down at me like I had just attacked his girlfriend.

She was crawling on the ground, struggling to find her sunglasses and keep her face covered at the same time. As she found them, he yanked her off the ground. She didn't quite have a good grip on the glasses and they went flying again.

~Did all of this make you angry?~

Of course it made me angry, but I was paralyzed. I couldn't move. I could see what was happening in front of me, but I couldn't stop it. I couldn't do anything.

~Why not?~

I don't know. I wanted to. I wanted to. Then I saw her eyes. For the first time, I saw her eyes, uncovered by sunglasses. They were so sad. They just stared at me, expecting me to do something, begging me to do something. I couldn't. I just sat there. I looked right back into those brown eyes and watched as tears swelled up inside them and fell, painfully, onto the bruised skin that those sunglasses usually covered. I couldn't do anything. I don't know why. I just couldn't. I . . . I . . .

~Do you need a Kleenex?~

No, I do not need a Kleenex. I'm fine. Just let me keep going or I won't be able to tell the whole story.

~Okay, so what happened next?~

He dragged her out by the arm. She kept looking back at me. I looked out at the tables and booths again. No one looked up. No one noticed. It was as if nothing happened.

~No one noticed a man dragging a woman out of a bar?~

Like I said, there weren't many people there. Besides, people have a tendency not to see things they don't want to.

~Or to see things they do want to.~

He dragged her out!

~Alright, he dragged her out.~

I was shaking. My hands were throbbing. I looked down to see they were clenched.

I felt a twinge of something I'd never felt before. It was deep inside of me. I can't explain the feeling, or exactly what it did to me, but it broke my paralysis. I got up and walked straight for the door. I knew what was happening outside before I even got to the door.

Outside, I saw them. The night was a little cold. They were the only people in the parking lot. He threw her inside of his red Ford and followed her in. Through the truck's back window, I could see their silhouettes. His silhouette reached over and smacked hers. My whole body shook. I breathed deeply. My hands were throbbing. The truck's engine started and its brake lights flashed.

I got in my Corsica and followed the Ford. It was driven to my apartment complex and barely stopped for her to get out. She tumbled to the ground. The Ford squealed off before she could even get to her feet. With her hands covering her face, she ran past the sign that read, Plain View Apartments, and into the complex.

~What did you do?~

I didn't know what to do. For a second, I debated about going to see if I could help her. It was too late by then. I missed the opportunity to help and I knew I couldn't face those eyes of hers again. I followed the truck. It went to a house not far from the Plain View Apartments. He got out of the truck and went inside the house. I watched as lights turned on and off inside the house, first downstairs, and eventually upstairs. I watched him through the windows whenever possible. If I couldn't see him, I watched the rooms that had lights on.

~You just watched?~

Yeah, I just watched.

~You didn't get out of your car and confront him?~

No. I just watched him. I started watching him regularly.

~You started stalking him?~

Stalking doesn't sound like the right word, but yes, I started following and watching him.

~When did you get the .38 Caliber revolver?~

It was the next day when he went to work that I went to buy the gun. I didn't know much about guns; but the salesclerk, Andy, was very helpful. Andy told me to buy a revolver, not a pistol. Apparently, everyone's first gun should be a revolver. Andy owned six guns: two revolvers, three pistols, and a rifle. He helped me pick out the S & W .38 Caliber Special. It was shiny and black with a four-inch barrel. I felt good holding it. It was heavier than I expected. It weighed about two pounds.

~.86 kilograms. I'm familiar with the gun.~

I couldn't actually get it until a couple weeks later. There was some paperwork, and a waiting period, and I had to put it on layaway. You know about that sort of thing, I'm sure.

~Yes.~

Meanwhile, I was following Mr. Bradley, Angel's boyfriend. I read his name on his mailbox.

~Matthew Bradley, Angela Errington's boyfriend?~

Angel! Angel's boyfriend. No, I suppose he can't be called that. She was a colonist and he was King Louise III.

~King George III.~

No, Angel was a Jew and Matthew was Hitler. That was their relationship. He wasn't her boyfriend.

~You saw him as her boyfriend and you wanted to be him.~

I never wanted to be him! He was pathetic. I followed him. I watched him. Everyday it was the same. There were only three things he did: he went to see Angel, he went to the bar, and he went to work. His life was pathetic. He was miserable. I never saw him with a single friend. He didn't have a dog or any kind of pet. All he had was the bar, Angel, and work. And he only looked at all content when he was with Angel, not at the bar, and certainly not at work.

Mr. Bradley was a security guard at Sears. I watched as he walked through women's intimate apparel and checked out every woman shopper. And he wasn't checking for shoplifting, either.

There was this girl in a red blouse and tight blue jeans. She had straight, brown hair like Angel's. She was looking at a white, frilly teddy. Mr. Bradley spotted her.

I was across the aisle, pretending to be looking for a scarf for my wife, or daughter, or mom, or someone. I moved closer when I saw Mr. Bradley approaching the girl.

"Finding everything okay?" he said. He stood tall in his blue uniform, with a whistle dangling from his neck. He added, "It's okay, I'm security."

She said she was doing fine and tried to go back to her shopping. But he wouldn't go away.

Then he says, "I watch to make sure no one is stealing anything."

The girl turned and he grabbed her arm. It was the same way he would grab Angel. That was the way he treated women.

~Maybe she was shoplifting.~

She wasn't shoplifting; she wasn't doing anything wrong. She never did anything wrong. If she didn't do what he wanted, he would hit her.

~He hit her?~

He hit her all the time.

~The girl at Sears?~

No, Angel!

~You weren't talking about Angel. You were talking about a girl at Sears. Did he hit her?~

No, but he would have.

~How do you know?~

He was about to, but then he saw me. I must have been careless and staring because he says, "What are you looking at?" He took his attention from the girl and she ran.

~Wait. I'm not getting a clear picture. He has his hand raised to strike this girl, when he turns and sees you staring at him?~

Well, his hand wasn't raised.

~Okay, his hand wasn't raised, but somehow you're sure he was about to hit her. Then he sees you watching him and the girl gets away. That just leaves you and him. You've been caught stalking this man; what did you do?~

I said I wasn't looking at anything. I held up a purple silk scarf and a red silk scarf and tried to say I was deciding on a present.

Mr. Bradley accepted this. He didn't seem to recognize me. Without another word, he reached down and picked up the white teddy and a matching bra and panty set. They must have fallen when the girl ran.

~Sounds like she was shoplifting. Why did you think Matthew Bradley was going to hit the girl?~

Because that's what he did. He hit. He hit Angel. The very next night after I saw her and him at the bar, he came to Plain View Apartments and picked her up. I don't know why Angel went with him. She was back in sunglasses again. A new pair. She couldn't be without sunglasses because he gave her black eyes. He hit her. I saw it. Every time he hit her, I jumped. It was always a surprise. There was no rhythm. He had no rhyme, no tempo. He was destroying her.

~If he was the one destroying, why were you the one with an S & W .38 Caliber Special? Tell me about July the fifth.~

I already started to. That was the day he saw me in Sears.

~It was getting too dangerous for you. You had to do something. Is that it?~

No. It wasn't about me. It was about her. It was about Angel. It was always about Angel. I couldn't let him destroy her.

~So you got your gun and you followed them to Mr. Bradley's house.~

They were in his living room. I could see them through his window. They were sitting on the couch. In front of them, on a coffee table, were two lit candles and a pizza box. I suppose he thought pizza to be a romantic food. She was nervous. I could tell.

~How could you tell?~

She was shaking as she ate her pizza. It caused her to drop some of her toppings off her slice.

~You could see that through the window? Where were you?~

In my car. I had binoculars. I could see everything. She shook as she ate and she dropped a sauce-covered pepperoni on the couch. Matthew looked at the couch, then back at Angel, sharp.

Bam. He hit her.

I jumped. Angel didn't deserve to be treated that way. No one deserves to be treated that way. But it was a regular thing for him to hit her. This time he hit her harder than usual. He hit her so hard I could hear it.

~How? You were outside in your Corsica and they were inside his house. How could you hear it?~

I just could, okay. My hands were throbbing. I was squeezing the binoculars with one hand, I looked down, and I was squeezing the revolver with the other. I brought my focus back to the house. I couldn't see them anymore.

~And that scared you?~

Yes. It scared me.

~What did you do?~

I don't know.

~Yes you do. What did you do?~

I got out of my car.

~The revolver was with you?~

Yes. The revolver was with me. I pulled its hammer back all the way and went to the door. I could hear her screaming and crying when I got there.

~But the door was still closed?~

Yes. The door was still closed. He was yelling, telling her to shut up and calling her names. I heard a smack. For a second there was no noise at all. I rang the doorbell.

The door opened and there he was standing in front of me. Mr. Bradley.

~Matthew Bradley.~

He must have hit her really hard. Angel had to lean against the white wall of the hallway, just beyond the door, as she approached from behind Mr. Bradley. She stepped next to him. Her eyes were barely open and those bruises! She had nasty bruises around her eyes.

Mr. Bradley's eyes were wide with surprise, staring at me and the revolver. My hand was throbbing and squeezing.

~You squeezed the trigger.~

No.

~Yes. You pulled the trigger. You wanted him dead. You meant to take his life. You pulled the trigger.~

No. I tried, but I couldn't pull it. I squeezed with my whole hand, but couldn't get my index finger to squeeze. It burned. The pain was intense. His eyes were huge as he looked at the gun.

~He went for the gun and you pulled the trigger. It didn't end quite as you hoped, but you pulled the trigger.~

None of that's true. He didn't move. He was paralyzed. I shook. I tried to pull the trigger. The gun was cocked. All I had to do was pull the trigger.

~You did pull the trigger! You did!~

I didn't. I couldn't. I whispered, "Third floor, please."

Then Angel's sad eyes focused in my direction. She smiled weakly as she saw me holding the gun. "Look Away." She spoke faintly.

~She told you to look away?~

No. That was the song she was humming on the elevator. It was Look Away by Chicago. When I heard her speak, everything stopped. My hand stopped hurting, my trembling ceased, and my grip vanished. The revolver fell. Then the gunshot came.

~You dropped the gun and then it fired?~

It was an eruption of sound. A dissonant clash of bass chords exploding like thunder in an instant, only louder and briefer, leaving only a single note, octaves above high C that lasted much longer.

You're saying it was an accident?

Mr. Bradley dropped to his knees as Angel fell to the ground. He grabbed her body and cried as he held her. She was his life that he abused, and he could feel it slipping away as he held her bleeding body.

I looked at her. She was smiling. She was at peace. An angel. Then she closed her eyes. I walked away. I freed her from Mr. Bradley.

~The gun dropped, then discharged and shot her in the sternum?~

I dropped the revolver. It fired.

~Matthew Bradley tells it differently.~

Mr. Bradley is a woman-beater.

~You stood there. You shot her. You dropped the gun. You murdered Angela Errington.~

I set her free. She had an unfair life.

~She did have an unfair life. But it was going great until a month ago. She was newly married to Jeffrey Errington, they leased a place in Plain View Apartments, and they were young and in love.~

There is no Jeffrey Errington.

~There was a Jeffery Errington. Then a month ago, they were coming home from Jeffrey's mother's house, where they had just enjoyed a family dinner. Jeffrey was driving their white Neon when he swerved to miss a German Sheppard that ran in front of the car. Jeffrey lost control of the vehicle. It flipped. He was killed. Angela Errington was lucky.~

I don't want to hear anymore about Angel.

~You're going to hear it. Angela Errington was lucky. She suffered ocular trauma and a concussion. She almost lost her sight, but the doctors performed eye surgery. It caused bruising around the eyes and extreme sensitivity to light. That's why she wore sunglasses all the time.~

She wore sunglasses because Mr. Bradley beat her!

~Do you want to know Angela's maiden name? It was Bradley.~

I don't want to hear anymore.

~Matthew Bradley is Angela's brother. He never laid a finger on her.~

He hit her!

~You imagined it. You imagined it all. You saw her in sunglasses and she intrigued you. You became obsessed. You saw her with another man in the bar and you became jealous.~

No.

~Yes! She stumbled, lost her glasses, and you saw the bruises.~

He beat her!

~You imagined it!~

He grabbed her arm at the bar!

~He loved her as a brother loves a sister! He led her out of the bar because she was still experiencing double vision from her surgery. It made her nauseous, and it messed with her equilibrium. That's why she stumbled. Not because of some abusive boyfriend. She needed to leave the bar. There was no abusive boyfriend! Only a dead husband.~

No.

~And you shot her. Dead.~

She smiled! She was suffering!

~She was suffering. But not as you imagined. You should have looked away.~

I saved her.

~You killed her. When the police arrived on the scene, the curtains were drawn on the house. You couldn't have seen in. You killed Matthew Bradley's sister in front of him.~

Mr. Bradley.

~Matthew Bradley.~

Matthew Bradley . . .

~Angela's brother. You went there to kill him. To punish him.~

To punish him, yes. Kill him, no.

~You brought the pistol. How else could you punish . . . Oh, I see. He was pathetic? That's how you put it? He had only one thing.~

Angel.

~You went there to take her away.~

He was nothing but dissonance.

~You murdered Angela Errington.~

I gave her harmony.

End.

I DIDN'T KNOW
by
Lisa Roberson

I didn't know it would hurt so bad
Or last so long
I didn't know that I could be so sad
Or feel so wrong
I didn't know they would look away
And leave me alone
I didn't know I would pay and pay
Never moving on
I didn't know I could hate so long
The things I've done
I didn't know

I began this anthology with an Ace of Spades; but, it doesn't matter how well you lead off, you still have to have something good at the end of the game to close with. So I'll finish this anthology the same way I began it. Here's a bonus story from our Featured Writer, Lynda Myles.

Myles is a master of the dynamic character. She knows how to hone in on that moment of change in a person's life. Her characters are complete with pasts and flaws. And while those pasts may be tragic and her characters are struggling, there is still a sense of hope in Myles' stories.

We, at J. D. Vine Publications, are not the first ones to recognize Myles' skill as a short story writer. The following short story was published online by The Jimston Journal. Here it is for the first time in print: *She Was Somebody's Baby, Too*.

SHE WAS SOMEBODY'S BABY, TOO
by
Lynda Myles

What woke me was that feeling you get when someone's watching you. I must've dozed off in my chair, because I opened my eyes and there she was, a little old lady in a purple caftan with giant pink flowers on it staring at me from across the living room. The robe was drooping off her shoulders, dragging on the floor, and she had a pink kerchief thing wrapped around her head like a turban. I wondered if Mo had a housemate living with her that the church people had forgotten to tell me about, someone who'd borrowed one of her caftans, since this was the kind of thing she'd wear.

"Didn't think you'd come," the old lady said in a raspy voice.

"Well . . . here I am."

"There's food."

"I saw, thanks."

She kind of sagged. "Excuse me – have to . . . lie down . . ."

Then she turned and felt her way out, holding onto the wall for support. I got up and followed her.

A couple of nights before this, a Reverend Knobeloch from St. Agnes' church in Akron had called me at my apartment in Albuquerque asking for Charlotta, a name I never use. He told me he thought I ought to know that my mother was dying of cancer.

"Did she tell you to call me?"

"Well, she— she told me she had a daughter."

"After you asked." It wasn't a question. "I go by the name Charlie, by the way, not Charlotta."

"Oh, I'm sorry. I didn't know."

Of course he didn't, I thought, since Mo always insisted on using that dumb name she gave me.

"Look, Reverend," I said, "I appreciate your calling and all, but see, I just started a new job, with a veterinarian? And it'd be real hard to ask for time off so soon?" I heard myself asking his permission not to go, which pissed me off no end. "And to be perfectly honest, I haven't seen my— Mo— for five years, and we didn't part on such great terms then. I didn't even know she was in Akron."

"Well, of course it's up to you, ah- ah—"

"Charlie."

"That's right. But people at the end of their lives often seek to—"

I cut into his sermon. "I'll think about it, okay, Reverend, and let you know?"

When I got off the phone, I was desperate for a drink. There it was, the old craving for that buffer between me and the panic, even after a year off the stuff. I thought of calling Terry, the guy I'd broken up with a couple of months before, but that'd be almost as bad as drinking. I gave serious thought to running out to buy a pack of Marlboros. I didn't have any around because I was trying to quit smoking. I knew for certain I'd have to get to a meeting that night. The woman was always screwing up my life, one way or another.

Her real name was Maureen, but everybody called her Mo, and I never lived with her. She left me – dumped me, depending on who's telling the story – with my father's parents right after I was born. Her husband, my dad, got killed in a car crash in Ohio where he was in college, when she was eight months pregnant. I popped out soon after, and Mo handed me over to my grieving grandparents, "just for a while," till she could get herself "on her feet." (Quotes by way of Aunt Tina, my father's sister, who never had any use for Mo.) Then she took her pretty, blond self off to L.A. to look for work as an actress. That's how I got lucky (for a while anyway) and ended up with my grandparents in Albuquerque. Lucky because they got to me in a big way starting from the first memory I have, which is of two or three-year old me, standing up in bed, puking and blubbering, while Nana held onto me and Grandpa cleaned up the mess. Then they sat close by till I fell asleep.

Next day I called Reverend Whatshisname and told him I'd be coming out as soon as I could arrange it at work and find a cheap flight. He didn't ask what made me decide to go, and I couldn't have told him if he did.

I met Mo for the first time when I was 18 at my first wedding (the marriage lasted thirteen months), and I only saw her four or five times after that. I may have been her closest living biological accident, but I'd spent maybe a total of a month with her out of my whole 39 years. Before my last visit to L.A., things had reached another crisis point in my life. I lost a good job managing a gift shop after I didn't show up for work a few times. Marriage number two had just ended. (Carson was a piano tuner and part-time psychic I met at a party. I didn't have a piano, but I had him do my astrological chart. We lasted two years.) I called Mo on a whim and she suggested I come for a visit so we could "talk girl-talk and figure things out."

Sounded good, but once I got there, it was the same old story. Every time I tried to open up the subject of my lousy life, she'd suddenly remember something she had to do right that second, like make an appointment for a touch-up because she had to look good for a big audition. She was in her 50's by then, so a big audition usually meant a commercial for a constipation treatment or whatever (how gorgeous do you have to be for that?). I got more and more miserable and spent more time in the bathroom drinking. Finally, I packed up and left without a goodbye. End of mother/daughter reunion.

Reverend Obi Wan Kenobi didn't meet me at the airport. Instead, a woman was there holding up a sign that said, "Charlotta." She was real small and cute, maybe 70, in a lime green pants suit, with bright white beauty-parlor waves and brick-red lipstick. I was dressed in my regulation uniform – jeans, a T-shirt – and my hair had expired during the four-hour layover in Detroit. But she greeted me like I was the most gorgeous creature she'd ever seen.

"Why, bless your heart, you're just as pretty as your mama!" She gave me a hug that bruised a couple of ribs. "I'm Mamie Hubbard. I worked with your dear mama on many church committees before she took ill."

"Thanks for coming to get me," I said.

"It was pure luck. The vestry meeting this morning got postponed on account of our secretary Rhonda's husband coming down with an attack of the gout. Of course, it wasn't so lucky for him, poor man. Here, honey, let me have that." She grabbed the strap of my beat-up rolling suitcase, the old kind you pull along like a dog on a leash, and took off with me practically running to keep up.

In the parking lot, we had a mini struggle over who would heave the case into the trunk of her shiny, spotless white Buick. She won. Then she barreled out of the airport and onto one of those roads with miles of fast food joints and car dealers.

"I wish you could've seen your mama when she played the Virgin Mary in our Christmas pageant," Mamie said. "She was absolutely ethereal."

"That must've been something," I said, trying to picture Mo as Jesus' mom.

"It was," Mamie said. "Of course, I only really got to know her well after her own daddy died -- your granddaddy -- she was so busy looking after him during his last days!" (Now I knew how come Mo had ended up back in her home town. For the same reason I was here.)

"But after he passed, well, she needed something to get her mind off her grief, and what with her theatrical background and all—" She suddenly took a hand off the steering wheel, grabbed my knee, and squeezed hard.

"Oh, I'm so glad you're here, Charlotta! I can tell you're just as sweet and nice as your dear mama. It'll do her a world of good to have you close by."

I mumbled thanks, even though I couldn't recognize Mo – or me – in any of this. For starters, I'm not sweet, and Mo hated her old man (that's what she always called him) and never went to church that I knew of. But I figured Mamie had staked out her opinions and wasn't about to budge off them for the sake of reality.

I set her straight on one thing. "I go by the name Charlie, by the way."

"Charlie? That's fun."

"Also, I need to get to AA meetings while I'm here."

I don't know what I expected, but not for her to look thrilled. "Honey," she told me proudly, "Akron just happens to be the birthplace of Alcoholics Anonymous. You didn't know that?" I shook my head. "Oh my, yes, it all started right here in Dr. Bob's house over on Ardmore, in 1935 or thereabouts. You really didn't know that?"

I shook "no" again.

"Well, we'll take you there sometime, it's open to visitors."

"Guess I've come to the right place," I said.

Mamie patted my knee reassuringly, "You sure did." The rest of the drive she filled me in on other highlights of Akron. Eventually, we wound up in a neighborhood of small ranch houses that all looked pretty much alike, till Mamie pulled up in front of one that was painted a kind of purplish blue with bright yellow trim, definitely a Mo color scheme. Mamie opened the trunk and slung my case to the ground before I could get to it.

"I need to have a cigarette before I go in," I told her. I'd bought some at the airport.

"Go right ahead, Lottie," she said, remembering I guess that I had a nickname, but not the exact one. "My late husband Norton used to puff away like a chimney, bless his soul. The smell of cigarette smoke always reminds me of him."

I didn't particularly want to know what had made Norton late, as I stood there sucking in deep drags. I stubbed out the cigarette and, when Mamie wasn't looking, palmed the butt and stuck it in a pocket. The street was neat and clean, and I wasn't going to be the one to mess it up.

It was dark in the house, till Mamie switched on a light. We were in a smallish living room, and if I didn't know it was Mo's, I could've guessed. There were wild-colored Mexican throws and rugs from her L.A. place covering the chairs and couch, hanging on the walls, and scattered around the floor.

"I just love what she's done here. So cheerful," Mamie said in a whisper. She pointed out where the kitchen was and said it was stocked with food, and there was a list of important phone numbers, including hers, taped to the fridge door.

This time I beat her to my suitcase and dragged it after her to a small hallway with doors leading off it. She pushed one in and I could see two single beds with faded red cotton bedspreads and red and black Mexican throws on them. Mamie motioned for me to set my bag in there, then she went to another door and nudged it open. The shades were down, a smell of stale air and antiseptic hit me. I could make out a mound in the bed. "Asleep," she mouthed, so we tiptoed back out to the living room where she put the house key down on a table. I panicked, knowing she was about to leave me there alone with the mound in the bed.

"The thing is," I said, "I don't know how long I can be away from my job—"

"All we can do is put our faith in the Lord, Lottie dear. I know you'll do the best you can." She gripped me in her iron hug again, gave a little wave, and left.

I stood in the middle of the floor wondering what to do with myself. What I was dying to do was call Terry, just to hear his low slow drawl melt all over me like warm chocolate. I got out my cell, plunked myself in a yellow serape-covered armchair and dialed his number, my heart flopping around in my chest like a caught fish on a pier. Then I had a sharp recollection of what he sounded like when he was busy with some woman and an old girlfriend called, and I pressed "end" instead of "send."

I took out the little photo of Nana I keep in my wallet and gazed at it. It knocked me out how much I still missed her. She and my grandpa raised me till I was ten, when he died suddenly of a heart attack. Two years later Nana got a stroke and only lasted a week in a coma. So at age twelve I was an orphan again. It was a perfect chance for bio-mom to come to the rescue, but she didn't have "the right setup" to take care of a kid. She was living in a studio apartment in "the Valley," making small change at clerical jobs and still hoping for a career in Show Biz.

I went to live with Aunt Tina and her husband Jeff in their house across town. They didn't have kids and didn't want any, but there was no one else around, so they won me by default. I was pretty miserable, but kept it to myself, so they wouldn't act more put upon than they already did. But I made up my mind to get out on my own as soon as I could. In spite of the fact that I was considered college material by some of my teachers, I took a full-time job when I graduated, got married, and left my aunt and uncle's house for good.

I guess I went off to sleep while communing with Nana's photo, because the next thing I knew the old lady in the caftan was there. I swear I didn't truly get that it was Mo till I went into the room and found her sitting on the edge of the bed where the mound had been. It blew my mind to think that this was the same person I'd walked out on five years ago. I was staring, my eyes prickling, looking for the woman I knew inside the face of this stranger. She was maneuvering herself to lie down. Finally, I snapped out of it and went to help her. It was weird touching her body, something I'd almost never done. She let me ease her back, lift her legs and cover her as if it was our normal routine. She stretched a scrawny arm over to the bedside table, knocking over some plastic bottles. "What do you want?" I asked.

"Pain pills . . ."

I checked out the bottles and saw one that said four tablets could be taken every two hours for pain.

"These?"

She nodded, I tapped out the pills, my hands shaking, filled up a water glass with a plastic straw in it, and helped her prop herself up to swallow them.

"Hope I can keep them down," she said. She leaned back with her eyes closed while I stood watching her. I was beginning to recognize her features in the mask.

The thing that was weird about Mo and me is that we looked so much alike. We had the same shape face, kind of squarish, same build, small-boned, except I was taller, the same color hazel green eyes, and the same pale skin and dirty-blond hair (when hers wasn't dyed gold or red). But looking at us you might not notice the resemblance right off, because she used to tart herself up, while I dressed like a construction worker (both descriptions courtesy of Aunt Tina). I'd seen pictures of her, but it was surreal the first time we laid eyes on each other in the flesh at my wedding in Albuquerque.

It was at Tina and Jeff's house. Mo drove from L.A. and got there late, so the pre stuff was over and the ceremony was about to begin. I saw her come in, dressed like a Mexican senorita, in a bright yellow, off-the-shoulders blouse, a red and black flare skirt, and cowboy boots. She looked great. She'd surprised me by accepting the invitation. Tina had promised to be civil to her, but she was so positive Mo wouldn't show that I hadn't really expected her. I'd only sent the invite as a courtesy, to let her know what was going on, the way Nana never failed to send her a Christmas card along with the latest photo of little me and maybe a crayon drawing I'd made. But she did show, and there she was, bigger than life and twice as colorful. I was wearing a plain white dress, my hair pulled straight back and sun-streaked. Hers was loose and beauty-parlor streaked. It was like looking in a funny mirror. We stared at each other, not smiling, not not smiling, just looking. Then I nodded, turned back, and kept on getting married.

The only thing I remember about the ceremony is that Dwight, my 19-year old groom, was already drunk as a skunk (like I would be soon), and I was in the same room with my "real" mother for the first time since I was a few weeks old.

Mo startled me again by opening her eyes and talking. Her voice wasn't so scratchy now. "Can you sit for a while?" she asked, as if I might not have the time to spare. I pulled up a chair. "How are you doing, Charlotta?" Oh, God, I thought, here we go again, Mo pretending to be interested. Her eyes were already a little glassy from the meds.

"Well, I have a new job, working for a veterinarian."

"What do you do there?"

"A little bit of everything, from feeding the critters to hosing out the cages."

"You like it?"

"Yeah, I like it a lot. I'm going to take classes, and he said if it works out, he'll train me to assist him." She was looking right at me, into my eyes. It was a heady feeling. I hadn't expected to get this far without her remembering the garbage had to be put out or something. "And I started going to AA," I told her. "I haven't had a drink in more than a year. Haven't stopped wanting one, though. I mean, I started on the stuff when I was thirteen."

"That young?" She sounded sad, which felt good.

"Yeah. I was drunk the first time I met you, at my wedding, and the last time, too, at your apartment. And every time in between." A warning ping flashed in my brain – back off, Charlie. But I ignored it. "It got so bad I couldn't keep a job."

"I'm sorry," she said, sounding really sorry.

My throat felt bone dry, but I kept going. "How come you never said anything about it the times I saw you? You must've noticed."

I guess I— I didn't know how to bring it up," she answered.

"I thought you just didn't want to get involved." This was farther than I ever got before with her in a conversation about us.

"No, that wasn't it." She reached her arm out, and for a crazy second I thought she was going to pat my hand, but she went for the water glass and took a sip. "I guess I thought—you know—" she said, "—that you'd tell me what you wanted me to know."

Cop out, I thought. "I tried a few times. You never seemed interested."

"That wasn't so."

"It always seemed like you had more important things to do than be with me." The pings were flashing all over the place now.

"That wasn't it, no—"

"I couldn't stop myself from pushing: "Then what was it?"

That's when she did this weird thing. She kind of faded out right before my eyes, like the picture on a TV screen dissolving into dots. Mo just wasn't present anymore. After a few seconds she shut her eyes and that was it. I stood there feeling stupid for a while, then went out to the front stoop for a smoke.

It was late in September, but it was still pretty warm in Akron, and the leaves were only starting to turn. There were some small flowers still hanging around, pansies maybe or petunias, I'm no gardener, but they looked bedraggled, like they knew their days were numbered. A kind of familiar, hopeless feeling came over me. Maybe Tina was right. When I told her where I was headed, she said, "Glutton for punishment, aren't you?" On top of everything else, she blamed Mo for my father's death. If Mo hadn't trapped her baby brother into a shotgun wedding, he wouldn't have taken on an extra job for the money, so he wouldn't have been driving home late at night after a rainstorm and gone crashing through a guard rail, down into a ravine. None of it would've happened if not for Mo. Of course, I wouldn't be here either, but Tina didn't seem to consider that.

I was in love with the adorable hunk in those photos I grew up with. My grandparents and aunt told me stories about Kenny, my father, how he was into carpentry from the time he was little and taught himself to build furniture and loved to read and wanted to be a teacher. I have a desk that's also a bookcase he built with his own hands when he was seventeen. It's still filled with his books – Gulliver's Travels, Treasure Island, Robinson Crusoe, On The Road, Shakespeare's Plays and Sonnets, The Brothers Karamazov, and lots of others. I knew he'd read them all because the margins were filled with penciled-in notes in his handwriting. By the time I was sixteen, I'd read them too, more than once. My notes were in pencil underneath his. The truth was I had a much better relationship with my dead father who I never met than I ever had with Mo.

After my second cigarette, I was still kicking around the idea of going home. I hated that every time I got near Mo, I couldn't stop wanting something from her. Like that first time at my wedding. She was the focus of the day for me, not my new husband. Everything about her fascinated me -- the way she held her shoulders, kind of defensively, the way she wrapped both her hands around her glass, like it might get away from her, the way her smile was a little lopsided. She was a one-woman show and I couldn't take my eyes off her, even though I pretended otherwise. I waited the whole day for her to say something meaningful to me, something important. But all she said before she took off was, "I hope you two will be very happy." Oh, and she left a big wrapped gift that turned out to be a toaster oven (which we used till Dwight threw it at the wall during a fight).

I lit up another one. I had to let go of all those "how come you"s and "you never"s, or there was no sense staying. Nothing Mo said or did could make a difference now anyway, it was too late. Just think of this as a humanitarian mission, I told myself. Hell, if you can tend and clean up after a sick dog, you ought to be able to do it for a sick woman. As long as you don't expect to have your face licked in appreciation. The phone rang inside. It was Mamie, telling me there was a meeting that night at seven and someone would pick me up at quarter to. That little woman was right on top of things.

When I got back from the meeting, Mo was in bed, awake. We were careful and polite with each other. She told me she'd taken some more pain pills and thought she could tolerate a little broth, so I heated up a cup for her. She held it with both hands wrapped around it and sipped. Then she puked all over herself. I didn't blink an eye, just helped her get out of bed, into the bathroom, got her cleaned up and changed into a new nightgown, put fresh sheets on and helped her get back in. I asked if she had any other kind of pain medication she might be able to tolerate better. She said no, but she wondered if I'd mind reading to her from the bible for a while. A surprise a minute, I thought.

"Sure." I picked up the bible on her night table and pulled up a chair. "Any particular part?"

"The Psalms," she said, "I like 57 and 63 especially."

"Okay." I found 57 and began to read: "Be gracious unto me, O God, be gracious unto me! For in Thee hath my soul taken refuge; Yea, in the shadow of Thy wings will I take refuge, Until calamities be overpast—" – etcetera. I read those two plus a whole bunch others, skipping over the parts about sacrificing animals and being brought forth in iniquity and conceived in sin by thy mother. When I finally looked up, I saw that Mo had drifted off. The tight lines around her mouth and eyes were relaxed. That went okay, I thought. I put the bible back, staggered into my room and fell on the bed. I was so wiped out by then I didn't even take my shoes off.

Mo was still asleep when I got up early the next day, showered, and threw the soiled sheets in the washer in the kitchen. She slept till the hospice guy came. His name was Jeremiah, and I liked him right off. He was kind of quiet, but friendly. Nice-looking too, with beautiful dark eyes. Probably gay, I thought. I went with him into Mo's room and stood back while he checked her pulse and blood pressure and spoke to her in a gentle way. She was different with him than I'd ever seen her. Her face became soft and—trusting is the word I'd have to use. She held on to his hand and looked like a little girl. I actually felt kind of envious watching them together, but I wasn't sure of which one.

Jeremiah said the doctor had OK'd morphine patches and showed us how to put them on. Then he got Mo into a chair while I smoothed the sheets and punched up the pillows. She was grateful. This'll work, I thought. I can do this.

After Jeremiah left, I heated up some more broth and she tried again. This time she didn't upchuck.

"Isn't Jeremiah wonderful?" she asked me.

"Almost too good to be true," I answered.

"He's the one who urged me to tell Reverend Knobeloch about you. He said you'd want to know."

"He's gay, isn't he?" I asked.

That threw her. "I don't think so," she said. "In fact, I was hoping, if you didn't have someone else . . ."

"I'm keeping away from men, for the sake of my mental health," I said.

"You're still pretty, Charlotta. You could find someone."

"I have zero luck with guys."

"Me, too. Except for Kenny. I always hoped I'd find someone else like him – so you could come live with us and we could be a family." She might as well have punched me in the gut. That lie made me so nuts I wanted to swig down a fifth of booze and hurl the empty bottle right at her straggly-haired, kerchief-covered skull. Instead I made myself take a few deep breaths.

"That's a nice fairy tale," I said finally. Mo looked hurt. Too damn bad, I thought and got out of the room fast.

The morphine patches helped her a lot during the next days, though she still had bad moments when the pain broke through. I kept her clean, put cold compresses on her forehead and read to her from the bible on request. Jeremiah showed up regularly and saved both of us from going crazy. It looked like I might actually pull this thing off.

Then one time I came into the room on one of her better days and found her propped up on the pillows, reading the bible on her own.

"You know, your grandfather was a very religious man," she said.

"He didn't go to church all that much."

"I meant my old—my father. He went all the time."

"Oh. Okay." I'd never met the "old man," so his religious habits didn't mean much to me.

"We didn't get along while I was growing up," she explained, "so I refused to go with him. But I took him when he was ill, and then I kept going after he died. It's been such a comfort to me."

"Great," I said, hoping she wasn't going to try to save me. I don't do organized religion. "Mamie said you played Mary in the Christmas pageant and you were very good."

She smiled, her eyes got brighter. "I have a picture, if you'd like to see it."

"Sure," I said. She told me to look in the bottom drawer of her dresser. There were a bunch of big envelopes in there with Mo's handwriting on them. I found one marked, "Christmas Pageants," but noticed another one with "Charlotta" on it. I took a fast peek inside – it was filled with cards, snapshots, and kid's drawings. I shut the drawer fast and brought the pageant envelope over to her. She slipped out a big photo of herself dressed in a white robe, her hair platinum blond, down to her shoulders, with a lot of makeup on. She was holding a doll wrapped in a blanket and gazing at it adoringly. The lighting made it look like she had a halo around her head. It was a super corny shot.

"You finally got to play a starring role." I joked. Mo's face kind of crumpled up. I thought she was in pain, but then I realized she was crying. I'd never seen her cry before. "What's the matter?" I asked her.

"Why did you come here if you hate me so much?" she sobbed.

I felt totally ambushed. "Why did you want me here?" I shot back.

"You're my flesh and blood."

"That was never a big deal for you before." I told myself to get out of the room and nip this in the bud, but this time I stayed.

"I didn't think you'd come all this way if you still hated me." Her whole face was wet and her nose was running. I shoved a box of tissues near her on the bed.

"I didn't think you'd ask me to come if you didn't have something to say to me." She looked confused. "Like what?"

"Forget it. It doesn't matter."

"What do you want me to say?" she asked. Her face was a puddle.

"Nothing, I don't want you to say anything." I reached over and pulled a clump of tissues out of the box and stuffed them into her hand. She still didn't use them.

"I told you I wanted you to come to live with me, Charlotta."

"Only if you found a guy who was willing to take me. Anyway, I don't believe you. You never said a word about it back then. And stop calling me Charlotta, okay? You know I can't stand that name."

She sobbed. "Why do you hate me so much?"

"I don't hate you!"

"Can't you forgive me, even now?"

"You mean forgive you for getting rid of me when I was two weeks old?"

"I couldn't help it, I was alone and afraid and I didn't have any money. I knew you'd be better off with your grandparents."

"You never came to see me, not once!"

"It was Tina, she told me I wasn't welcome."

"You didn't have to listen to her! You didn't even come when Nana died." I could feel the burning behind my eyes. But I'd never cried in front of her and I didn't want to start now.

"I didn't think you wanted me—"

"I was a twelve-year old kid. I needed somebody who cared about me."

"I was only five years old when my mother died," she whimpered.

"She couldn't help dying. It wasn't her choice!"

"But the old man never really loved me."

"At least you had a father." I reached over and grabbed a handful of tissues – this time for me.

"You had your Grandpa Ernest." she said.

"He died when I was ten, for chrissakes!" It hit me – we were having a cry-off over who had it worse. I could've laughed if it wasn't so pathetic.

"Please don't take the Lord's name in vain."

"Jesus Christ, give me a friggin' break! I know you found God all of a sudden, but have you asked Him to forgive you for abandoning your kid?"

"I didn't abandon you, Charlotta, I brought you to your grandparents. Try to understand, I didn't know what do after Kenny got killed. It's terrible to lose someone you love like that."

"Yes," I said, "I know exactly how it feels."

"But I only had him for such a little while."

"Longer than I did. And you could've had me." There, I'd said it. After a bit, she started up again, in a small voice.

"I wish I'd been stronger. But I tried to make it up to you—"

"You did? How?"

"I tried to be your friend after we got together, but you wouldn't let me."

"I wouldn't let you?"

"You were always angry at me."

"Bullshit!"

"You were angry at me every time I saw you." Her face was flushed and she was speaking fast like she had to get the words out before something stopped her. "You said mean things to me every time. When I drove all the way to Albuquerque for the wedding, you know what you said to me? You said, the way you're dressed, you must've thought we were getting married at a rodeo."

"I never said that! Maybe Tina did, but I loved the way you looked."

"It was the first thing you ever said to me, I swear on my immortal soul!"

"I did not!"

"It's true! And when you introduced me to Dwight, you told him, 'This is my mother, the wannabe Hollywood starlet.'"

"That's such a complete crock!" I couldn't believe she was throwing this wild stuff at me now. When I quit drinking I had to go around and apologize to people I'd dumped on. But I never thought for a second I owed Mo an apology, not in a million years. Not after what she'd done to me. Even if I had said some mean things to her when I was drunk.

"Those were your exact words. I swear on this bible!" She slapped her hand flat on her bible. "Your exact words, so help me God. I felt so awful, I wished I hadn't come."

"Why the hell did you come, after staying away for 18 years?"

"You invited me, so I thought you wanted me there. I drove all the way from L.A. to Albuquerque—"

"Big eff-ing deal! You want a medal because you came to your only child's wedding?"

"I never said I wanted a medal!"

"Then what the hell do you want from me?" I was yelling.

She yelled back, "I want you to be nice to me!"

"I have been nice to you, goddam it! What do you think I'm doing here?"

She broke down again, weeping. "But I need you to love me, you're all I have. I know God loves me, but—but I thought if you came—it meant you could love me after all."

I couldn't stand it another second. I reached over, took the tissues out of her hand and wiped her wet, snotty face. I had to say "Blow" to get her to help.

"I'm scared, Charlotta." Her voice was hoarse again, croaking, "I'm so scared—"

That's when it finally dawned on me that I'd been beating on a door with nobody behind it. I wanted to stay mad at Mo – mostly because I didn't know any other way to feel about her – but, I thought, what's the use? If one of us was going to give in, it had to be me. Otherwise she'd die, and that'd be that. The only big message Mo had for me, that she'd ever had for me, was that she was even more scared than I was. For the first time I actually felt sorry for her, sorrier than I did for myself.

"I'm not going anywhere," I said. It was all I could think of to say, but I felt a need to put my arms around her and try to make her feel safe. So I did.

End